EMPTY

EMPTY EARTH

JACQUELINE DRUGA

PRESS

VULPINE
PRESS

Published by Vulpine Press in the United Kingdom in 2022

Cover by Claire Wood

ISBN: 978-1-83919-398-9

www.vulpine-press.com

Thank you all to those on my Patreon that walked the
Empty Earth with me.

ONE
NOT DEAD

Sometimes death is better.

It isn't always the easy choice, but often it's the only choice. The only choice we *think* we have.

I wanted the pain to stop. Not a physical pain, although it had manifested into that as well. A part of me didn't even want to die, but I felt it was what I needed to do. I really couldn't live with it any longer.

Was it the quiet that stirred me, the smell, or just the fact that I had been out of it?

What was that smell?

But I woke up.

Alive.

I wasn't supposed to. That wasn't the plan. My eyes were heavy, hard to open. I had to blink several times to see; they were dry, as if they'd been open the entire time.

Was I alive?

I truly felt dead.

My body was in a weird position on that couch. Legs twisted, one on the floor, the other tucked under my backside My chest was flush against the cushions, one arm dangled downward, the other bent awkwardly behind me.

Cheek pressed against the rough fibers of the fabric, top of my head smashed into the arm of the couch, I tried to move.

My back and head hurt, and my mouth was so dry, when I tried to move my tongue, it felt like there was something lodged against it, bits and pieces of something, then I realized…there was.

I spat something out as I tried to lift my head, my cheek was glued to the couch with my own dried vomit.

That was what was in my mouth. Dried vomit.

I'd regurgitated in my passed-out state. Had I been on my back, I probably would have died.

Then again, that was what I was aiming for.

It was gross and disgusting. I scraped off the vomit from my cheek and as I sat up fully I knew that wasn't the only bodily substance that had been released from my body.

Yeah, that smell was me. I was the reason for it.

I was a mess.

I cringed because I failed.

The prescription pill bottle was on the table next to the pint of vodka.

I wasn't supposed to die. I was meant to face my consequences.

There would be no pity for me, not even in my state.

I didn't deserve pity.

My phone rested on the table.

The sleep screen was on.

I thought back to when I took those pills. I thought it was enough, certainly washing it down with vodka should have done the trick.

But it didn't.

I wasn't trying to take the easy way out, I just wanted out.

I reached for my phone; I was alive, and I needed to at least right a wrong. I had to let Louis know I was okay. After all, he was the one and only person I texted.

I put in my passcode and opened my phone. I saw I had nine missed calls from Louis. All in a row and all after my ominous text. I remembered a couple of those calls coming. Wanting badly to answer, but not wanting him to talk me out of it. It was too late anyhow, when I sent him the text, I had already swallowed the pills.

It was a matter of waiting.

I opened my messages. His text message thread was first.

Louis: my soon to be ex-husband.

When I opened the message thread I stared at the last text I sent him.

Five words.

I just can't. I'm sorry.

That was it.

His reply as just as short, '*Viv, WTF*'

And that was before he started to call me.

I thought about what I wanted to text him now. Maybe something like, 'I was an asshole, hope you aren't upset.'

What I wanted to write was that I was sorry, and I needed help. But I knew that would be taken as me making some sort of excuse. I was certain his girlfriend was probably telling him I was just vying for attention.

I wasn't.

I just wanted someone to know I was done, and I was sorry.

He was all I had.

The only person on the earth that cared enough even though we had split up.

In the middle of texting him I saw it. The message date-stamp right by my last message to him.

Sunday, April 4. 10:04 pm

It didn't say 'yesterday' which it should have, considering in my mind it was no more than twelve hours since I sent the last text.

I closed the messaging window and looked at the home page of my phone.

The left corner of my phone displayed 7:32 AM. Then my eyes shifted downward to the calendar icon.

Tuesday, April 6.

What?

Not only had I been out of it for nearly thirty-six hours. It was D Day. The day I didn't want to face, the day I wanted to die before I faced.

Death had eluded me; I had to face the music.

There were two and a half hours remaining for me to clean up and get downtown for my hearing.

I stood from the sofa, everything stiff, from my legs to the clothes I wore. There wasn't much time to clean up, I wasn't even sure I'd be coming back. It could be the last time I'd see my house.

Coffee was all out, I had to get myself together and meet my lawyer at nine. I would stop at the convenience store for one.

In the bathroom, I guzzled water from the tap before brushing my teeth. I still felt dizzy, I knew it wasn't from the pills. There was no way they were still in my system. I charged my phone while I was in the shower. Not that it would make that much of a difference, but it would give me enough power until after my hearing.

Seeing how I was such a hot mess, I did my best to look decent.

Washing the crud from my body took longer than I expected.

I never imagined that on the last day that I might see my house for a while, I would be racing out.

Yet there I was, a quarter after eight, grabbing my purse and keys as I rushed to the door.

Reaching for the handle, I froze. My hand shook out of control, and fear took over my entire body.

This was it.

How long would I be gone?

My reckoning.

It took nearly a year to get to the point I was at. A year of torture, trying to forget, unable to get it out of my mind.

It would never leave my mind. No matter how much I tried or paid, the punishment was forever living with it.

Perhaps that was why I so badly wanted to die.

TWO
RECKONING

When it happened, I was in such a horrible space, I blamed everyone. Louis, the traffic light, a blind spot.

It was crazy how your mind goes into self-defense, looking for reasons that could explain what happened. That would justify why my mind screamed out, 'No, not me, this isn't me.'

But it was me.

Louis hadn't come home again. The third night in a row, he stumbled into the house in the early morning and passed out on the couch. He kept saying he was done, it was time to move on. But how do you just do that after twenty years together?

Just...move on.

In hindsight it was a lot longer than those three days, but in my mind at the time, it was all new, all fresh.

That morning, before I left for work, I lifted his hand and used his finger to open his phone. He didn't even know. He was out. I knew snooping wasn't good and I undoubtedly would see something I didn't want to. Sure enough, pictures of him and Renee all through his phone. Text messages of love and other things.

I didn't know her name at the time, or who she was. Just that she looked as if she were barely old enough to drink.

I tried waking him to argue, but he didn't care. He was nonchalant, almost relieved that I knew.

I stormed out of the house, in some dramatic fashion: crying, screaming, acting like an idiot.

"How could you do this to me? Why would he do this to me? Why? Why?"

I wasn't even halfway down our street when I picked up the phone and called him. Three rings and it went to voicemail.

I turned left onto Murken Avenue and dialed again.

Not even a ring.,

"Are you kidding me!" I shouted. The anger, the hurt. How could he not even want to talk to me?

Six more times over the six blocks on Murken, I unsuccessfully tried to call. Then I commanded my phone, "Send a message to Louis."

I rambled and ranted, forgetting punctuation.

Send.

Then the moment came.

I replayed it, you know, over and over. Wanting badly to have something different happen. A different outcome.

No amount of replaying it would change it.

I was driving on West Lincoln Avenue. The main drag in our little borough. Four lanes during rush hour. Two lanes with street parking when it wasn't. A hot spot at night for young college kids to hang out. Lots of bars and restaurants all down the road.

7

The stoplights were every block and if I paced it right, I never had to stop. I caught every green light.

I had driven that road to work for eight years. The speed limit was twenty-five, it was rush hour and I was going thirty.

Thirty wasn't fast, right?

Bleep.

My phone alert went off.

It rested on top of my purse, and I shifted my eyes to see it was from Louis.

I didn't know what the message said; I swiped my finger to read his two words.

'Just stop'

How fitting. How ironic. What if I would have taken those words verbatim at that second? I freaked out when I saw it and started texting my reply. I had my eyes away for a split second … a split second.

That was enough.

When I looked up, I saw her.

She was right there at the hood of my car; I swore her eyes connected with mine and she knew. She knew before I did.

I wasn't even fast enough to hit the brakes at that second. Not that it would have mattered. I did more than strike her, I plowed through her. She flipped up cracking the windshield and rolled over the top of my car. I could hear the thump of her body as it careened across the roof.

My foot didn't even slam down on the brake until she was over my car. By that point I was thirty feet away and she was a body in my rearview mirror lying limp on the road.

My immediate reaction was panic. It didn't happen, it couldn't have. Begging in my mind that it wasn't real, I peered in the mirror again. A crowd had gathered around her.

8

I lifted my phone and called 911.
"What is your emergency?" the operator asked.
"I just killed someone."

That moment, that precise moment was the most honest I was for a long time. I kept trying to deny it. Make excuses.

I was so blind by my own selfishness and rage. Blinded by what happened and how it was going to affect my life, I never thought about what my reckless actions took from others.

Stephanie Miller was her name, she was nineteen years old.

A full life ahead of her and I stole it because I couldn't keep away from my phone.

I robbed her mother of a child.

I felt guilty at first, then camera footage showed that the light wasn't working. Stephanie had the crossing signal at the same time that I had the green light.

I didn't run a red light, she didn't cross against the light.

I had an out and I was taking it. But then the guilt came back when I saw her mother in the courtroom, a look of agony on her face that would never go away.

Enough was enough.

The truth was, I was at fault. Had I been going the speed limit, not looking at my phone, I would have seen her.

The moment I admitted to texting and driving, it was like a lynch mob. Every person that knew Stephanie stood before the judge and talked about how my selfish, reckless behavior caused them grief and they'd never be the same.

I got it.

I felt it.

Every single day I saw her face, I heard that sound when the car hit her. It played in my mind constantly, waking me from dreams.

My sentencing hearing was about to take place and my judgement was at hand.

No amount of jail time or punishment was enough.

Guilt over what I had done consumed me.

Yet, I stood at my front door terrified to leave.

Finally, I did.

My insides trembled and my heart raced out of control. It would be over soon.

I turned onto Murken and that was when I knew something was wrong. It was rush hour and the streets were empty.

At first, I thought my phone had been wonky and maybe it was wrong. Where were all the cars, the steady stream of traffic?

It was a six block drive from Murken to West Lincoln and in addition to the lack of traffic, the stop lights were flashing. Still on automatic.

Thinking that maybe I was wrong, that the pills had caused some sort of residual delusion, I pulled over right before the turn on West Lincoln.

Since the accident, I kept my phone and purse in the backseat.

My plan was to check my phone for the date, then call my attorney and tell him I was on my way. I put the car in park then reached back for my purse. When I did, my fingers grazed the strap and I knocked my purse to the floor.

Shaking my head in disbelief, I opened my door and stepped out.

I took a second to look around because it felt weird. No sounds, no cars. It was so strange. A part of me felt I was dreaming or maybe I had died and I was living in some sort of strange hell or purgatory.

Reaching for my back door, I paused to close my driver's door, just in case a car came, and that was when I saw him.

A man laying face-down in the beginning of the cross-walk at the intersection of Murken and West Lincoln.

It looked as if he just dropped over.

Hurriedly, I opened the back door, grabbed from my phone and raced his way.

He just lay there, a take-out container with spilled food was by his head.

"Hey!" I cried out to him and immediately called 911.

It rang and rang.

No answer.

"Are you kidding me?" I ended the call and dialed again. It was ringing when I arrived at the man's side. It was then I noticed that the spilled food looked old and smelled bad.

Phone to my ear listening to the endless ringing, I crouched down and reached to him and that's when I realized the smell wasn't the food, it was *him*.

His body was hard, and what I could see of his face was purple and splotched.

"Help!" I screamed out and stood. "Someone?!"

The line rang.

Racing out, I believed my answer was West Lincoln. It was a main drag, it was rush hour, someone had to be around.

Ringing. Ringing.

I wanted to throw my phone.

Why wasn't anyone answering?

It took only stepping onto West Lincoln and I knew something bigger had happened. It went beyond the man on the street.

The man wasn't the only one.

Several bodies were strewn across the road, some on the sidewalk. A car had driven straight into the front window of Bethe's Bar and Grill; under the rear wheels were two more bodies.

Another car had struck a telephone pole and beyond that it looked like a chain reaction smash-up.

There were no sounds.

Dead silence.

Dead everywhere.

It wasn't real. It couldn't be. I stood on that street in a complete state of shock.

"Please dear God, let me be dreaming. Please let this be a dream." I muttered to myself.

I knew it wasn't.

THREE
BACKTRACK

It had to be me. What I witnessed, what happened around me could not be real. It had to be a product of my imagination.

I was either still sleeping or having a hallucination. It was also completely possible that I mentally snapped.

My life had been a roller coaster for ten months. The last few, after admitting my guilt, I faced not only Stephanie's family but myself with the truth, and it wasn't freeing, it was internally damning.

But I deserved it.

We lived in a small borough outside the city, and everyone knew nearly everyone.

I couldn't go to the store without someone staring, watching me.

I started going to the next town for something as simple as gas.

I couldn't, nor did I want to, show my face.

Friday had been the victims' statements. It was all day; I couldn't believe how many people made statements. From teachers, employers, to friends and family. The only family members that didn't make an impact statement were Stephanie's grandparents.

Stephanie's father made sure he mentioned them. How the grandfather would die of a broken heart because Stephanie was his lifeline.

Every statement, short or long, was like getting struck with a baseball bat to my chest.

My lawyer wrapped it up by reiterating I was a good person that made a mistake. He told the court how I had lost my job of ten years, my friends, and even my husband.

I wished he wouldn't have done that. I didn't want sympathy, I wanted whatever punishment was to come my way so I could say, 'Okay, this is what I need to do to move on'.

That wasn't going to happen, I didn't think, not any time soon. Before the hearing, I tried to move on to normalcy, but any time I smiled or laughed, Stephanie came to mind.

Louis may have left the marriage, but he did not leave me as a friend. He was there, every day. He had moved only a few blocks from me and would walk over to make sure I was alright.

Perhaps he felt some inkling of guilt as well.

The mind is a strange trap that can pull us into itself.

Which was exactly what I believed was happening.

I have had dreams I couldn't wake from. Dreams that would continue even if I woke up and went back to sleep.

Surviving an attempted drug overdose and waking to a silent world with dead bodies?

It couldn't be real.

I had to backtrack, go back home and start again.

I drove slowly, looking around. Everything seemed empty and quiet. No one walked the streets. So many porch lights were still on. No one was alive to turn them off.

The quiet was frightening.

I had never experienced such fear in my life. It was like walking through a haunted house, waiting for something to jump out. My heart was beating so fast, there was no way to control it. I felt in a fog, unsure of my own sanity.

When I turned from Murken onto my street, it was a different view. No longer something in my rearview mirror I failed to see.

An ambulance was parked, rather wrecked, into a fence, in the front yard of a home two houses from my own. How did I miss it?

I stopped in front of my house and immediately started to race to that ambulance, but I stopped.

A spiderweb crack spread across the windshield.

I didn't want to see inside. I knew.

My house was where I had to be.

I was worried and scared, and the unreasoned person inside of me kept thinking I was going to be late for my own sentencing, as if the events around me weren't a valid excuse.

Home was my safe zone. Go back to the beginning, go back to the couch, reset.

I don't know what I was thinking, just wishing everything was wrong.

If it was my imagination or a hallucination then it was very real, because when I opened that front door, the horrendous smell blasted me.

I wanted to believe I didn't notice it when I woke up, that it really didn't smell different, but it did.

My stomach churned, glands swelled with salivation, I wanted to vomit.

Vomit.

I saw the couch.

The few whole pills that were evident in the dried puddle of regurgitation.

All of the sudden I was pelted with a memory of something. It took me out of the 'now' and transported me somewhere.

'Come on, Vivian, don't do this. Vivian, come on,' Louis' voice. His voice, begging, blasted at me in some sort of audible flashback. *"Vivian please."*

Gag.

Vomit.

"That's it. That's it. Just hold on."

Was I remembering?

I walked closer to the couch, staring down to the pills. There were less there than I consumed.

Like a drunk slowly reconciling his blackout, specks of that Saturday night were coming back to me.

'Come on, Vivian, don't do this. Vivian, come on. Vivian please."

A hard pressure to my jaw, something entering my mouth, pushing down against my tongue, scraping the back of my throat causing me to gag.

I remembered throwing up.

'That's it. That's it. Just hold on," Louis said.

Black.

Oh my God, I panicked. Was Louis there? Was he there that night?

The feeling of ill continued, there was nothing in my gut to throw up, yet, I kept retching, uncontrollably Saliva filled my mouth, then poured from between my lips.

Everything spun.

I raced to my kitchen to get some water, to splash my face, something to snap me out of it.

I made it two steps into my kitchen before I realized the nightmare had only just begun.

Lying on my kitchen floor was Louis.

FOUR
PIECES

No. No. No!

I sobbed, cried out, dropped to the floor, grabbed on to the man that I had loved for more than half my life.

"I'm sorry, Louis, I'm so sorry," I told him.

It didn't matter.

He didn't hear me.

It was clear that Louis had been dead for at least a day or two. His skin was hard and purple, parts of it split like a stressed seam to a pair of jeans. He was so much like the man I saw in the crosswalk. Louis' open eyes were bloodshot red, and there was a thick coagulated blood under his nose and on his ears. I didn't notice if the man in the crosswalk was the same.

I didn't look at him like I looked at Louis. I didn't know the sidewalk man. I knew and cared for Louis so I saw everything that the event did to him.

In his hand was the phone, clenched there tight within his rigid fingers, the screen was black.

The way his legs were twisted, body turned, it looked as if Louis just dropped.

Like the crosswalk man.

My first thought was he was there. Louis was there with me.

But what happened?

The screen on the phone was black and I pulled it from his hand.

Touching the screen woke it from its sleep state and I tried his passcode.

He had never changed it.

I quickly learned he held on to that phone because he had called 911. A call was placed at 10:16. nearly fourteen minutes after I texted him.

He'd rushed over.

The call log told me he was on the call for nearly two hours, that was the length of it. But he had texted Renee in between.

I looked at his message.

She had been the last person he spoken to. Probably messaging her while on hold with emergency services.

One text message. At 10:30. 'Found her. Pills. 911 on their way. I got her to throw up. It's not good.'

He called for help, he sent a message to Renee. I wondered if the ambulance just two doors up was really meant for me.

They didn't make it.

Louis didn't make it.

No.

That was not reality.

I couldn't fathom that something so devastating had taken place here. Something so horrible, that in a span of two hours wiped out every single living person. There was no way. No.

Louis wasn't dead, neither was that man in the street. There had to be another explanation.

When I was a teenager, I had a dream that I was walking through a small town, and everyone was gone. Once in a while I would see someone, and they were decrepit, suffering, and quiet. My mother was convinced that I had somehow been transported into another dimension, one where damned souls wandered.

A little heavy-handed, but then again, my mother was a minister.

I thought of my mother and that dream. How it felt surreal.

I decided at that moment to shuck the sadness away. It wasn't real.

I didn't change my clothes or shoes that I was going to wear to my sentencing hearing, there was no need.

Instead, I decided to walk, play along with the hallucination or dream.

I moved down my street to Murken, figuring the more I moved the better chance I had of snapping out of it.

I needed to get beyond the last point, that intersection with the body and the car smashed into Bethe's Bar and Grill.

The body was still there, same position, the takeout container spilled. It was wings, the sauce dried, and shriveled.

"You're not real. None of this is real," I said, pausing as I stood just over his body.

It was then, staring at the Buffalo Wings, that I heard it ... music.

Roy Orbison, *Pretty Woman.*

"Are you serious?" I chuckled. My delusion was getting more ridiculous by the second. Figuring I was game, I followed the sound of the music.

It took me to Bethe's and I stepped inside.

Not far from me, seated two seats from the end of the bar, was an old man. His back was to me, but I saw the reflection of his face in the mirror behind the bar. He was maybe eighty, with thinning white hair that was tossed and messy. A bottle of whiskey sat in front of him, and he nursed a neat drink and smoked a cigarette. An IV pole, with an empty bag, tilted against the bar, the line of which led into him. He wore only a hospital gown, tight up top in the back and wide open exposing his naked back and rear end as he sat on the stool.

I stared at him for a second, he didn't move or budge other than to sip that drink.

I smirked and felt better, "Okay, now I know none of this is real."

Then he looked at me.

FIVE
REALITY

The old man glanced over his shoulder at me twice, finished his drink and hit his cigarette a couple of times.

I didn't move.

He did.

After setting the cigarette in a makeshift ashtray, he stood up. His skin caught against the vinyl of the stool making a squeaking noise as he slid off.

I cringed.

Rear end fully exposed, he grabbed that IV pole and walked to the jukebox. To be polite I immediately looked away when he leaned over for the plug. He pulled it and silenced the music.

"Knew that would work," he said. "Noise carries in the silence. Like sneaking in the house at night, damned if you don't make noise." He walked back over to the bar.

I looked at that IV and the empty bag as he set it down..

He noticed I was looking at it. "Yeah, I should remove this IV. Do you know how? Are you a nurse? Nah. You're not dressed like a nurse."

"I … I am."

"You're what? Dressed like a nurse?" he asked. "I may be old, but I don't think I ever recall nurses dressing like they're going to a job interview or court date."

My eyes widened when he said that. "I um ... was going ... never mind," I said. "I'm a nurse. Pediatric nurse. Not in a hospital. A Quick Med."

"Ah," he sat down. "Well, you know, I'd appreciate if you would unhook me."

I nodded, then stepped to him and stopped.

"What is it?"

I didn't answer.

He sighed out. "It's real. All of this is real. I heard what you said when you walked in here." He pushed the bottle. "Grab a glass."

I didn't budge.

"You really are convinced this isn't real," he said, spinning on the stool enough to face me. "You think I'm a delusion."

"Well, in defense of my sanity," I said. "Finding you here like this is kind of crazy."

"So, you think you're dreaming."

"That or I entered another plane."

"Another plane?" he asked. "Like an alternate universe."

"Yes."

"This isn't DC Comics, toots. It's real."

"It could be hell," I said.

"It's not hell."

"Purgatory?"

"I am not in hell or purgatory, I can assure you of that. Unless God has some screwed up scoring system, I'm pretty sure I aced his every test. Why would you think it's hell or The Spiderverse?"

"Because I did something really bad," I replied. "And just before I woke up to this I took a bunch of pills and washed them down with vodka to kill myself."

He whistled. "Well, now you're gonna make me rethink this all."

"Really?"

"No. It's real. This is no outer world experience or LSD trip," he said. "It's real. I came-to just as the last of my attending team rolled from my gurney to the floor."

"If it's real —"

He slammed his hand. "It's real. Everyone is dead. Everyone."

"Then why aren't we?"

"Luck, timing. I think it's because we were already dead when it hit. That's my guess. I don't know. I just wandered here and had a seat at the bar. Figured if I put on the jukebox, anyone alive would hear."

It was real? Everything was real?

Suddenly everything I avoided feeling, the worry, the sadness, and shock all pelted me at once. I turned for the door.

"Where are you going?"

"I have to see," I replied. "I looked at everything like a delusion, now I have to look at it knowing it's all real."

As I headed out, I heard him mumble about removing the IV line. I would get to it. But first, I really needed to face the truth.

I suppose I expected some sort of epiphany when I stepped back outside. Maybe I would see everything in a different light, break down in tears, feel devastated, but I didn't. It just felt real. I wasn't telling myself it was a dream or drug induced.

I stayed out there for a little bit longer, expecting the old man in a hospital gown to join me. But he didn't.

When I went back in, he was pouring another drink.

"Feel better?" he asked.

I shook my head and sat down next to him. "I don't feel worse. I feel empty."

"Yeah, I faced that yesterday."

"I find it sadly ironic that I wanted to die and leave this world, only to try, and find myself still here with everyone dead."

"I don't know what to tell you."

"You're not gonna say there's a reason."

He scoffed a little. "No. I always found that if you're gonna say that line, that things happen for a reason, then you better damn well have an inkling of what that reason is." He extended his hand to me. "Stan."

I grasped his hand, it was warm, his skin fragile and some of his knuckles were large from arthritis. "Vivian. You can call me Viv."

"Viv. Nice to meet you. Wish it were under better circumstances, but it's nice to meet you." He lifted his drink to me then took a sip.

I watched him sip that whiskey and hit that cigarette, two things I was willing to wager he gave up years beforehand but took them up after recent events in a 'what the hell' fashion.

We were two strangers. But considering the circumstances, we wouldn't be strangers for long.

SIX
BAR TALK

There were bodies in Bethe's. Aside from the smell, I really didn't notice them at first, I was so focused on the half-naked elderly man drinking at the bar.

The longer we sat there the more I saw them.

Two at a booth, another at the pool table, three by the dart machine. I found the bartender when I went behind the bar to see if there was a way to make coffee.

The pot was behind the bar, and I found the grounds in the kitchen. The ovens were still warm, and I tossed a couple bar pizza's in there. Stan needed to eat, he said he only had crackers the last two days.

My mind spun with a ton of questions, but I didn't want to ask him everything all at once. I also didn't want to force him to leave the bar. I envisioned him having some sort of emotional connection to it.

"Nope," Stan replied when I asked him. "Never been here."

I placed a band aid over where I removed the intravenous line. "Really? How did you end up here?"

He glanced down to the fresh bandage then back up to me. "I saw it. I needed to stop."

"When was that?"

"Yesterday, evening I think." He lifted the crinkled plastic wrappers. "Where'd you think I got the crackers from?"

I smiled gently at him and pushed a plate toward him. "Eat your bar pizza."

"Thank you," he said, taking the plate

"Are you from around here?" I asked.

"Not really, I lived in Caudwell up until about four months ago when my wife and I went into Springs Retirement Community."

"Wow, that's a nice place. Years ago, when I was doing my clinicals, we did a shingles vaccination clinic there. It's like a hotel, and the good was really good.:

Stan nodded. "It is. I had some pain in my thigh after church on Sunday, they sent me to the hospital a few blocks from here."

He fiddled with the crust of his pizza.

"That's more than a few blocks," I said.

"Oh, who's counting. Anyhow I went."

"Blood clot?" I asked.

"Wow, you're good. See a lot of blood clots with the kids?"

I smiled again. "No, just figured that's what it was."

"Me, too. I have these varicose veins, figured one of these days they'd do me in." He lifted his bare leg. "See?"

"Yep."

"They did me in and saved my life. Not sure that's all a good thing." He took a bite of his pizza. "Not bad."

"Thank you. So, you obviously died," I said. "But not for long?"

Stan shook his head "Not for long. When my eyes popped open, one nurse was lying half on my feet the other half on the gurney, and she just rolled off. I laid there for a while, calling out for help, listening to the insanity."

"What do you mean?"

"Oh, Viv. When the world just drops dead it doesn't go in a whimper. Car crashes, explosions. So many car crashes." he said. "I finally realized no one was coming. I got up. Fully expecting to, you know, just drop dead. It happened so fast. I spent that entire evening walking around that hospital. Trying to figure out what happened. But this is a puzzle. There are no newscasters or doctors to tell us. This is something, if we want answers, we're going to have to find them."

I peered around the bar. The blank televisions, the bottles still on the shelves. I didn't know where he thought we would find those answers.

"Do you think it's everywhere?" I asked.

Stan nodded. "I do. If it was just us, surely help would have come. Strange thing is the electric is still on, the phones."

"Won't be for long."

"No. No, it won't be." Stan seemed unfazed about anything he witnessed. "There was a nurse on her cell phone when it happened. Phone was plugged in, charging. She was chatting away. Whoever she was speaking to had met the same fate."

"How do you know?" I asked.

"Because when I looked at that phone before I left, she had been on the same call for sixteen hours."

"Wait. Sixteen hours?" I watched him nod. "Must be different with 911. They must automatically disconnect."

"Why do you say that?" he asked.

"Because my ex-husband died at my house calling to get help for me. The call ended after two hours."

"Maybe they do have some automatic thing. Or maybe someone ended the call."

"At the call center?" I asked.

"Or your house." He shrugged. "You never know. Part of that mystery you and I have to unravel. Are there others. We'd better hope there are. I'm an old man, if we don't find others, that's a lot of life left for you to spend alone."

"Stan, do you think there are others alive?"

"I do." He nodded. "In fact, I know there are at least three others."

"Oh my God, you saw three other people alive?" I asked excitedly.

"I did."

"Where?"

"At the hospital. On life support. But they won't do you any good." He took another bite of his pizza, finished his drink, then stood.

"Where are you going?"

"I think it's time to find some clothes. I'm feeling a little drafty." He walked a few feet and stopped. "You coming?"

I slid from the stool, and hurried to walk beside him. I didn't want for a second to lose track of the only other person alive. I looped my arm through his, sure it was support for me as much as it was for him.

He moved slowly, his gown flapping open with each step, but that was okay, I wasn't in any hurry to see what was outside again.

SEVEN
INTERMEDIATE

The shiny, royal blue, two piece running suit certainly wasn't something I expected Stan to pick out, yet that was what he chose from the plethora of items at Treasure Gold Resale. In fact, he grabbed a green one as well.

There were a lot of shops located on West Lincoln, all shops we could walk to, but there were also a lot of bodies.

We had to break a window to get in, the alarms blared for about twenty minutes then stopped. I just wanted off that street. If we needed anything, there were plenty of places outside the crowded borough we could drive to. Considering whatever happened had occurred on a Sunday night, traffic would be sparse.

He had one more shop to break into.

It made little sense to me as to why he needed me to throw a brick into the door of the real estate office. I thought, like with my first impression of him at the bar, there was some sentimental attachment.

Then he explained: "we need a place to stay tonight or for however long while we put together a plan. I don't know about you, but I want a plan, even if it's to ultimately go swimming in a swamp in our skivvies, I want a plan. And I know you're thinking about being generous with your house and all-"

"No, really, I wasn't, it's a mess and my ex is there. Well, his body."

"Exactly. We need a place with no bodies. A vacant place."

"Wow, that's really good thinking Stan."

"Thanks." He nodded. "They have the keys that open those lock boxes. We need one."

"There's a vacant house on Murken and Price. It's big, too."

"Let's shoot for that. Now break that window."

I lifted the brick, the same one I used at the resale shop, and aimed it.

"Wait!" He called out, "stop."

"What?"

"Someone's in there. Well, dead, but still." he reached for the door and pushed it open. "How about that? Good thing I checked before you went crazy and smashed the place up."

I followed him inside. A woman had died at her desk. She slumped half out of it, her head facing down.

"That's a good worker," Stan said.

"How do you know?"

"She was here on a Sunday night."

"Maybe she was having an affair."

"Maybe not everybody sucks and cheats on their spouse," he said, walking to her. "Go check the back for a cabinet with keys."

"How will I know which key is which, should I grab them all or are they marked?" I asked.

"We're looking for a lockbox key, they're universal. I'll check her purse."

I had no idea what he meant about a cabinet. Was it a file cabinet, some cup cabinet? I had no idea where to even begin looking. That ended up not being an issue.

"Found it. Janis had a key."

I stopped and looked back, he held up a set.

"You knew her?" I asked.

"Who?"

"You said Janice had the key."

"Her, yes." Stan nodded as a point to the body. "I didn't know her personally." He held up a business card. "Really nice picture of her. I wouldn't even bother looking at her face now. Head's been down like that."

"Can we go?" I asked. "Please."

"Yeah, I'm ready to stop for the day."

I was surprised Stan did as much as he did. I wished he didn't and was glad to hear he was ready to rest. While I didn't know him, he was the only other person around and I didn't want anything to happen to him. I joined him at the desk and together we walked out.

He carried his resale shop bag with his spare jogging suit and Janice's purse. I wasn't sure why he grabbed that, but I was certain I'd find out.

<><><><>

There were several things needed before settling into the corner house for the night or however long we'd be there. It was vacant, and while there was power, there was no food. I

33

wanted to find some, and I wanted to go back to my house to get a few things.

Not much, it wasn't like I had a lot back there. I wanted my car and to change my clothes.

I made sure Stan had a bottle of water and a bag of chips to hold him over until I got back. He talked a lot about making a plan, I didn't know what that entailed, but I was open to talk about anything.

I asked him if there was any medication he took daily. At eighty three years old I was certain there was medication he needed. He said he didn't, I didn't believe him. Just like a part of me didn't believe him when he nodded and said he'd stay put while I went back to my house.

In a strange twist, I had originally tried so hard to convince myself nothing was real that when I found out it was real, I forgot how bad it was at my home.

I didn't mean just Louis' body, it was everything about who I was and what brought me to this point.

I was slapped back to the reality that I was trying to escape the world that had evolved around me. The endless nights of guilt and crying, hating myself for what happened, and dreaded days that I would never escape it.

Not that I ever would, but the world I tried to leave was gone.

Everyone I hurt, damaged, ruined on that one fateful day was now gone.

Dead.

There was no one to atone to, no one to apologize to or to allow to see justice served.

They died without that peace as would I.

I didn't waste time at my house. I changed my clothes and grabbed a few other clothing items along with my phone, Louis' phone, and only a couple memorabilia items.

I couldn't bring myself to go to the kitchen to grab food, but I did go down to the basement to the storage freezer and gather a few items from there. It was enough to get us through a day or so. I didn't see us staying very long in our town of Beaumont.

There was no reason to.

EIGHT
STEP ONE

With everything that I wanted to take from my house stuffed into a small gym bag and one grocery store tote, I drove back to the house.

It was four in the afternoon, and I could see the sun already dimming. I looked at my gas gauge, there was only a quarter tank of gas. Knowing we needed electricity for gas and not wanting to take a chance of the power going out before I could fill up, I turned one street before Murken and headed down to the Quick Fill a few blocks away.

There was one car in the lot of the Quick Fill, it was the night worker's. Very few people got gas there, especially on a Sunday evening. I parked by the tank and tried my credit card in the pump, surprised it didn't authorize and, dreading it, I went inside.

I didn't see the clerk at all, the internal music system played, and the empty store was eerie. I expected him to be behind the counter, but he wasn't.

Maybe he was in the back, or the cooler; I wasn't searching him out.

I had worked at a convenience store years beforehand and knew how to authorize a pump. I slipped behind the counter and to the pump computer and authorized it for a large amount, enough to fill up.

I just wanted to get out of there. Get gas, get back, and shut the day out. Plus, I didn't like leaving Stan for that long.

After filling up, I left and hadn't made it four blocks before I swore I saw someone on a bike.

It was hard to see because they turned the corner. Hurriedly, and with excitement, I picked up the speed.

Another person alive.

My heart raced and when I turned the bend I saw the bike rider. He peddled quickly but kind of weaved about. It wasn't another survivor, it was Stan.

Slowly, I pulled alongside him.

"Are you running away?" I asked.

"No." He stopped. "I wasn't sure if that internet google stuff was working and we needed research. He pointed to the back of the bike and the carrying basket there. "I went to the library to get books."

"Where did you get the bike?" I asked.

"Funny thing. I started walking and I saw it on the ground. Well, near a body, so I grabbed it. Made things faster."

"You shouldn't be riding a bike, you died a couple days ago. Or your heart stopped."

"So did yours," he replied.

"I'm not eighty."

"Neither am I. I'm eighty three. See you at the house." He immediately began to peddle again.

"Stan," I called out, but he ignored me.

He was stubborn, but I knew he was also really strong.

Keeping my speed slow, I stayed close behind. I wasn't letting him out of my sight.

"Can I ask you a question?" I set a bowl of soup before Stan and a small plate with saltine crackers. That's what he wanted, something light and not heavy before bed.

"You can ask."

"Do you have any family?"

He lifted a butter knife, taking the tiniest bit of butter and placing it on his saltine as he obviously delayed answering me. He glanced my way as I sat at the table with him.

"You're not eating?" he asked.

I took that as an answer to my question. "I will. Not yet."

"Probably a late snacker," he said, bit his cracker that swooped his spoon into the bowl. "Yes," he said as he took that first spoonful of broth.

I thought maybe he was making a comment about his soup until I realized he answered my question.

He had family.

His reluctance to answer told me not to push any farther.

"You?" he asked. "Other than your dead ex-husband."

"No. Well, maybe some cousins. No one close. No siblings, my parents passed on a couple years ago."

"No children?"

I shook my head. "Sadly no. I wanted kids really bad. A whole slew, you know. A bunch running around, but Louis couldn't so we *didn't*. Now ..." I started to make the comment about how it was a good thing but refrained since I didn't know Stan's situation. "Now, I just think."

"Slew of kids is good. Not always at Christmas and not always when money is tight. Maybe you may still have some." He took another bite of his soup. "But don't look at me for that."

I coughed out a chuckle. "Okay, I won't."

"You're not going to ask me any more questions?"

I shook my head. "No. You can tell me what you want and when you want to tell me."

"We have time for that, don't we?"

"We do."

"Did it cross your mind that maybe all the dead out there are gonna get up at any second?"

His random comment took me aback. "I'm sorry, like resurrection? Book of Revelation stuff?" I asked.

"No, like Train to Busan stuff. World War Z."

"Zombies?"

"Yes."

"No." I shook my head. 'It didn't occur to me."

"Just thinking about it. You know, part of that plan."

"Do you have a plan?" I asked. "I mean mine is kind of vague. I'm still processing everything. Just long term survival, you know. I was thinking about that."

"Yeah, that is kinda vague. You gotta be more specific. If we're not, we'll be bored out of our minds in no time. Now, you don't have to pay any mind to what I want, but eventually we look to see if there are more survivors. It's Spring. If there's no survivors we have plenty of food out there to last us for a while, but we'll need to do any planting and such."

"Looking for others crossed my mind."

"It's something to do," he said. "But to me, the number one thing to work on is answering the big question."

"The big question?"

"Yes. What is the big question? What's the first question that comes to your mind when you look around?"

"What happened?"

Stan snapped his finger and pointed at me. "Bingo."

"We both died. Anyone else that beat this thing died as well. We missed it."

"But don't you wanna know?"

"We'll never know."

"We'll never know if we don't try," he said. "It's a shame, you know." He glanced up. "The lights are on. The world sort of stopped. You would think, with all the technology still lingering around out there, that there has to be a way to see what happened."

"Technology. Yeah ..." I said in an almost dazed state. My mind started racing with ideas. "There might be." I pushed his food closer to him. "Finish your soup."

NINE
LIGHT, CAMERA

Something as simple as a storm brought the end to modern conveniences, at least in our area. Just after dinner the storm rolled through. Stan meandered around the house looking for candles, I didn't understand why, after all it wasn't that bad.

Then the thunder began to intensify as did the wind and lightning and as my new friend predicted, the lights went out.

I found myself thinking it wouldn't be long before they came back on, until I realized there was no one around to flip the switch.

Fortunately, the house was furnished on the first floor and Stan made a bed on the couch..

I sat in the den, comfortable on the window bench seat, eating a cup of soup and staring out of the bay window into the darkness. The only time I could see beyond the edge of the lawn was when the lightning flashed. The thunder was loud, the rain steady. It was pretty scary. Especially when I started getting inside my own head.

Suddenly, in the dark, Stan's zombie question wasn't so crazy.

What if he was right? What if the dead did rise? We had no weapons, nothing to defend ourselves.

Would they be textbook zombies from movies or something completely different?

Whatever they were, we needed protection.

Immediately I thought about that umbrella stand in the foyer and the baseball bat I saw in the holder. I set down my cup of soup and ran for that bat. It would work. I returned to the den and reclaimed my seat on the bench.

It was a great house. Much bigger than mine.

I hadn't gone exploring yet, I didn't want to like it too much. We wouldn't be staying. Then again, Stan's plan to talk about 'a plan' went to the wayside when he grew tired.

It would wait.

The day was long, really long.

I woke up two days after I took a handful of pills to find everybody dead and a new way for me to pay for my mistakes.

I thought a lot about what Stan had said about how he wished we could see what happened. I had some ideas, none of them would work if the power was out everywhere.

Settling into some sort of zone, I finished my soup and relaxed. I wasn't sure if I would be able to sleep since I had slept so long.

I fell into some sort of daze, watching the horizon, or rather the edge of the property where the world seemed to disappear into an abyss. I watched the flashes, looking for lurking figures to appear like in a horror movie.

There was no color outside, just black and white.

I thought maybe it was best to blow out the candles. If the dead were outside and waiting to attack, surely they could see us.

We were a target.

Flash.

I looked, nothing but tree branches and outlines of dark homes across the street.

Deciding to blow out the candles, I stood.

Flash.

Shit.

My heart fell, there was a figure, standing across the street. A male figure.

There. Gone.

My heart raced.

Fearful, I peeked again. I didn't see him in the dark and passed it off as my imagination until the lightning lit everything again.

He was there.

This time closer. The rain falling steady on him, and his arms were slightly outward in some sauntering zombie attack mode.

I screamed.

A short scream.

Hurriedly, I locked the window, grabbed the bat and raced for Stan.

The second I stepped from the den, Stan was there, causing yet another fright and scream.

"Good heavens, what are you screaming about?" he asked. "And put down that bat."

"You were right," I said, rushed and panicked. "There's a zombie. They came back to life."

"Oh, nonsense."

"Come see." I dragged him to the window.

He seemed irritated and then the lightning flashed.

"What am I looking at?" he asked.

No one was there.

Silence.

Bang. Bang. Bang.

Three hard knocks came at the door, causing me to jump and scream.

"Oh my God." Stan grabbed his ear.

"See? See? I told you someone was there."

"It's not a zombie, they wouldn't knock."

"Don't answer it."

"I'm answering it."

"No, stop." I tried to reach for him. "At least take the bat."

He waved his hand at me and walked to the foyer. He peeked out the panel window next to the door and glanced my way. "It's not a zombie."

I stood behind Stan as he opened the door.

A man stood on the porch. His shoulders moved up and down quickly, as if he were scared and breathing heavily. He was soaking wet and his long, drenched hair came just past his shoulders. His head was slightly lowered. He wore a uniform, like a bus driver or something, it was hard to tell.

After another flash of lighting, he slowly raised his eyes. His lips quivered and he looked genuinely spooked.

"Please," he said. "Please tell me you're real and alive."

"We're real," Stan said. "We're alive. Come inside."

Stan opened the door wider and the stranger walked in.

TEN
OPERATIONS

The sudden appearance of the wet stranger at the door was something out a slasher film.

We had nothing warm to offer him except water and a little whiskey from Stan's bottle.

Dennis Nash was his name, and he didn't have another pair of clothes. Despite how badly he tried to hide it, he shivered from being cold.

I offered him a blanket, he accepted.

"Thank you. Thank you so much," he said. He kept pushing his hair from his face. But every time he glanced down to his cup; the wet strands fell forward again. "I thought I was losing my mind."

"Me, too," I said. "I thought it wasn't real."

"I never doubted it," Stan added. "How did you find us?"

"This part of town is dark, so even a little light can be seen," he replied. "I was on the tenth floor, back at work, looking out, looking for life when I saw the lights and I followed them here."

Stan asked. "You've seen no one else?"

He shook his head. "No. I tried, you know? This afternoon I swore I heard music. I tried to pinpoint the direction. I followed it, but it stopped. I knew someone was alive."

"What happened to you?" I asked.

"Freak accident. Freak timing," Nash replied. "I was at my job. Just came on for my night shift. I went back to the kitchen to make a coffee, but something was wrong with the machine. The last thing I remembered was reaching for the plug. I felt a pinch. Next thing I knew I was on the floor with Miller on top of me." He looked at me, probably noticing the confusion, so he clarified. "He must have been doing CPR because the CPR mouth guard was still in my mouth. and he just fell forward over my chest."

"So, you died, too," Stan said.

Nash nodded. "I guess I did. But I was hopeful because there were still active calls happening. I thought maybe it was an attack on our building, some sort of freak gas leak."

"Where did you work?" I asked.

"I work at a PSAP," he replied. "A public safety answering point. Or emergency call center."

"You're a 911 operator?" I questioned.

"Yes, that's how I knew there were several calls still connected," he said. "So, I tried reaching out. I noticed that some were hours old. Which meant I was out for a couple hours."

I nodded. "You ended the call my husband was making."

"If it came into our center, I ended the call, yes," he replied. "No one was there. No one answered. I couldn't reach anyone anywhere, and I tried. Trust me I tried. Nothing. I raced home … I went home and that was a mistake."

"Your family?" Stan asked.

"My wife, kids." Nash closed his eyes painfully. "I can't process it. They were all in bed. And now." He trailed off.

"What about you?" He was looking at Stan when he asked that question.

"I have family. A wife. Six kids. Fourteen grandchildren and nine greatgrandchildren," Stan replied. "I have them. In my mind right now, Bess, my wife, is making a warm milk to calm her nerves with this rain. Everyone else is doing their thing, you know. The little ones are probably in bed. Bess always gets up when it storms. Funny." He shook his head with a smile. "I have not gone home. I like to think that I left them, left them the other day without any word. Went to the store to get milk and didn't go back. I'm not gonna go back, at least not yet. That's my mindset."

I reached over and squeezed Stan's hand. "I like your mindset." Another squeeze and I exhaled, turning to Nash. "So, you work in a pretty secure place. Bet there's cameras."

"There are," Nash replied.

"Did you look?"

"For what?" he asked.

"To see what happened, when it happened."

"No, I didn't."

Stan snapped his finger. "Vivian, that's a great idea. We can see what happened. See how long it took!"

I nodded. "Exactly. That's what I was thinking. I wanted to see if we could find some sort of camera system. Is the power still on at your building?"

"It is," Nash replied.

"Can we go now?" Stan asked.

Nash shook his head. "It's really dark and dangerous out there. I'd advise waiting until morning."

"That's what we'll do," I said. "First thing we will head over there and check out the cameras, that way we can see what happened in that office building."

"I can do you one better," he said. "I'll show you the city."

ELEVEN
A VIEW FROM ABOVE

I wished I could say I had a good night's sleep, but I didn't think I'd ever sleep well again.

It was hard after the accident to sleep without medication, now the world was gone and really, what did it matter. It was as if I was a prime candidate for the apocalypse. A ready-made hell.

What did I lose?

Other than Louis, I lost absolutely nothing.

All of my friends abandoned me after the accident. They didn't want to associate with me, so I guess they weren't friends. The closest thing I had to a friend was Louis' girlfriend. She genuinely worried. that night, when I tried to take my life, she responded to Louis that she was on her way.

Somewhere out on the car-strewn road, in her ugly rust colored VW, was Renee.

Then again, we didn't know what time exactly it happened, but we would.

We took my car to the emergency call station. A building located just before the outskirts of downtown. It took a lot longer to get there because we had to weave in and out of side streets.

We ended up having to park on the road. It was easier to walk to the building than waste gas and drive around.

It wasn't as if someone was going to steal my car.

The main drag before the building reminded me of a child's toy car collection. Just random smash ups and calamity.

It was just baffling to me. People got in the cars, none the wiser of the devastating fate that waited for them. They drove, died, and crashed.

Every car was something different.

Some looked as if they merely drifted into another car, others looked like they were going full speed ahead.

Bodies just weren't behind the wheels, some were through the windshield, on the ground, twisted and broken.

The ones that died in their car looked in agonizing pain.

Life sucked from them.

They just stopped living.

We were about to see it happen.

I didn't know if I was ready, but I knew in order to move forward it was something I had to see.

I had to know.

The parking lot had a lot of cars, which wasn't surprising. The event happened around the change of shift.

Nash led the way into the building.

As soon as we entered you could smell the dead bodies. Of course, two security guards were dead right out front.

"This way," Nash said and walked by the elevator.

"Are we taking the stairs up?" Stan asked,

"Actually, we're taking the stairs down," Nash replied. "The CCTV center is four stories below. It's there in case of emergency."

That made sense.

We took the stairwell all the way down, there was still another level below where we exited.

A big thick metal door opened up to a hallway lit by overhead lighting. Emergency lights were every twenty feet. We passed a cleaning cart. As if he had done it before, Nash swiped up the can of Lysol and tossed it my way.

"We'll need that."

I could only assume he meant for the bodies, but I didn't think it would work.

We walked down that hall until we came to the CCTV room.

For some reason I expected some high security area. But it wasn't. The walls were glass with partially open blinds and the door had a large window.

There were three people inside ... all deceased. They had been sealed in.

A feeling of dread overcame me about opening that door. I didn't want to be hit by what I knew would be a horrendous odor.

It wasn't like a bad cooking odor or walking into someone's house that had a lot of cats. Those smells, no matter how bad, were ones that you got used to.

Not the dead.

That smell didn't go away. It got worse and would be horrible until they reached the point of decay where they didn't smell any more.

I covered my nose and mouth, while clutching my disinfectant can. I took in a breath and held it when Nash opened the door.

Stan grunted a sound of disgust. Nash winced.

Even in the doorway, I couldn't bring myself to go in.

Speaking through my covered mouth, I said, "I can't go in there, I'll watch from here. It's gonna be too bad."

"Yeah, well, it will be just as bad in the hall," said Nash.

I didn't know what he meant until I saw him rush in, grab a chair with a body and roll it out.

Once he stopped, the bloated body of the worker slid from the chair, and this long stringy substance followed. Like rubber cement, it pulled and stretched.

Seeing that caused my stomach to churn. I fought to not vomit.

I had never seen a dead body before in my life. Never did I expect them to look like that. Bloated, discolored.

Once the last body was out of the CCTV room, I was in there like Quick Draw McGraw spraying that Lysol disinfectant spray, hoping it would mask some of the odors.

It didn't make it better.

Reminded me of a public restroom when someone tried to cover a bad bowel movement with perfume.

Disinfectant and rotting bodies were a bad combination.

But the smell faded to the back of my mind when I looked at all the screens.

There were so many, and I felt like I was in some sort of apocalypse sci-fi movie. Each screen was black and white, no sound, no movement, only dead bodies and destruction.

"Do we know when this happened?" Nash asked.

"Between ten and eleven," I replied. "Two nights ago." My eyes cased the screens.

"There," Stan said. "Monitor Twenty-three, that's Bethe's Bar and Grill. Focus on that one. I think two men were outside when it happened."

He knew there were two men outside because they were run over by a car.

I knew that much.

Knowing the area, the camera had to come from the corner stoplight. A traffic cam.

It was a perfect and slightly distant shot of Bethe's.

It was nail-biting. In fact, one arm crossed over my waist as I brought my fingers to my mouth and watched. My eyes shifted from the time stamp to the images.

Sunday 10:04 PM

Three men stood outside. A minute later a woman joined them. They laughed, smoked cigarettes. The two men went in, another came out.

The woman chatted with them. A few minutes later three more men came out.

I supposed it was the way things were at bars. People congregating outside, smoking, talking.

Then at seventeen minutes after, only two men remained. One in a tee shirt, the other in a hoodie. Not able to hear what they discussed, I imagined they spoke of sports, hockey maybe.

They laughed. They got along.

A third man came back out. He wore a baseball cap. He didn't speak to the other two, he stood off to the side.

Other than their conversation nothing was happening.

We had no option but to watch. It wasn't as if we had anywhere to go. We had time.

And the minutes clicked by. Then, twenty-eight minutes after, the man in the hoodie spun counter-clockwise, losing his balance.

Tee-shirt man reached for him, but hoodie-man's knees buckled.

Tee-shirt man looked as if he called out for help, spinning for baseball-cap guy who, too, had fallen to the ground.

Bright lights suddenly illuminated the front of the bar.

Tee-shirt man dove out of the way as a car careened into the front of Bethe's.

The car pummeled hoodie and baseball cap man.

The one in the tee-shirt wasn't seen.

"Back it up," Stan said. "Can you play it again?"

"Yes," Nash answered.

What was he looking at?

As if he could see it better, Stan moved closer, focusing only on that monitor.

He watched what I did. Two men dropping and a car plowing forward.

"Did you see that?" Stan asked. "If you watch them both, the man in the hood and the man in the baseball cap, they fall, they die, seconds apart. Did you see?"

"Yeah, okay," I said.

"Nash, back it up again," Stan requested. "Stop it when the car plows in. If you can."

"I can. I can slow it down," Nash said.

"Please."

"Why are we watching this again?" I asked.

"Just watch," Stan said. "We'll call the man in the hood Man One. The guy in the hat is Man Two, the other guy is Man Three."

The video replayed.

"Man One down …" Stan narrated. "Man Three reached for him but look, Man Two is down. Here comes the car. And …stop."

The image froze just before the car crashed into the bar.

Stan pointed. "Man One and Two are on the ground, the car rolls right over them. Man Three is gone. He jumped out of frame and out of the way of the car."

I nodded. "Alright, yeah he did."

"You aren't getting it, are you?" Stan asked. "Man One and Man Two dropped dead at the same time, probably the same time as the driver of that car. But Man Three didn't. He didn't drop. He beat this thing and dove out of the way."

"We beat this thing," Nate replied. "So, Man Three beat it. He lived."

"Again, missing my point," Stan said, shaking his head. "We all beat it, yes. But we all died to beat it. Man Three didn't die. He beat it and is alive out there. If he is …" Stan said. "Others are too."

TWELVE
MORE THAN WORDS

Where did he go?

Once it sunk in what Stan had said about Man number three, my mind raced, and I was trying to look at the screens.

Which screen went with which camera on Main Street?

He jumped out of frame. Did he run, duck in a building?

There was only one more CCTV traffic camera on that street and unfortunately it was two blocks away. The man in the graphic tee-shirt, the one Stan nicknamed 'Bub', bounced out of the way of the incoming car, out of the camera's view and went *somewhere*.

"Can't we tap into Bethe's camera?" I asked. "I mean they do it on TV."

"Yeah, unfortunately, it doesn't work that way," Nash said. "We can't tap into a camera. We can go to Bethe's and see if we can find their system."

"More than likely," Stan said, "He went into some panic mode, then went searching for everyone he knew. We can try Bethe's, not sure how that camera stuff works. But chances are, he's long gone."

"Or," I added, "he's holed up somewhere."

Nash shook his head. "No, he's out looking for someone. Anyone. That's what I was doing, that's what we all were doing."

"But at this point, he knows everyone is dead," I said.

"So, we look for him," Stan suggested. "We do like I did with the music, only we find a way to broadcast a place for him to go if he hears us."

"Like a PA on a police car," Nash replied.

Stan nodded. "Exactly."

"We can do that,' I said. "It's still early in the day. We can drive around and look"

"We have to make a plan," Stan added. "That was the plan for today, to make a plan on what we're going to do."

I pointed at the screens. "We are. We're looking for him."

"And that covers tomorrow?" Stan asked. 'The next day? We need a plan. For starters, I don't know about you, but I don't want to live in ignorance or at least ignorance from not trying."

Nash asked. "What do you mean?"

Stan pointed at the screens. "I want to know what happened to everyone. At least try to figure it out."

"How?" I asked.

"You." Stan nodded at me. "You're a medical professional."

"I'm a pediatric nurse."

"You're still a medical professional. We get one of these bodies before they get too bad and we try to figure out how they died," Stan said.

"Like an autopsy?" Nash asked.

Stan nodded. "Exactly. She can do it."

I laughed.. "I'm a pediatric nurse. I don't know the first thing about an autopsy."

"Well," Stan flashed a closed mouth smile, "good thing for you I went to the library."

Stan thought it would be a good idea to give me the book he found while Nash searched out the camera source at Bethe's.

"Autopsies for Dummies?" I read the title. "For real?"

"Yeah, I thought that was a pretty good one when I saw it." Stan set down a cell phone and opened the cover. "It's like everything you need to know about doing one."

"And then what?" I asked. "How am I supposed to know what's wrong?"

"Book tells you everything. What a healthy set of lungs looks like, check out page sixteen." He flipped to the page. "Look at that. Surely, you can tell the difference between a diseased organ or good one."

"And do what with that?"

"Well, okay, you cut someone open, and their heart is huge, maybe blown apart, then we know that's what killed them. We cut open a second to confirm—"

"Whoa. Whoa." I held up my hand, "I'm not cutting into two people."

"You need to."

"No." I shook my head. "I don't."

"Sure, you do. You need to confirm."

"And where am I supposed to perform these autopsies?"

"At the morgue," Stan replied. "I'm sure they have everything you need." He closed the book. "Vivian, I don't have many years left and I don't want to spend those few years wondering what happened to the world. We have to at least try. For you that's a heck of a long time of not knowing. And by the time you figure out that you do wanna know, it'll be too late to try."

I exhaled heavily. "Fine."

"That's the spirit." He lifted the phone again.

"Where did you get that phone?" I asked.

"At the booth over there. I missed it earlier. It's dying. It needs charged."

"So, you're just looking through some random stranger's phone."

"Sure. Why not? Everyone's lives were tied to one of these." He held it up. "I'll add to the others I have."

"Why?"

"It's just something I want to do. I'll explain it some time."

"Sounds strange," I said. "Not as strange as an autopsy."

"You're gonna do it though, right?"

I nodded. "But we look for Bub, the tee shirt man first."

"Deal."

"If we can figure out which direction to go."

"Guys," Nash came from the back, "I think we might be able to figure out who he is."

"Hot damn," Stan said. "Ask and you shall receive."

"I got into the cameras." Nash walked behind the bar.

"Grab me that bottle of Old Grandad, will ya?" Stan asked.

Nash paused, sought the bottle and handed it to Stan.

"What did you see?" I asked. "Can I see?"

"Sure, but there weren't that many people here, right?" Nash asked. "He must have been new here because," he walked to the cash register, "even though it looks like he came in with the first guy that got hit by the car," he continued, opening the register drawer, "they took his license and credit card when he started a tab." He reached in the drawer, then turned and set three licenses and credit cards on the bar. "He's one of these."

"Him." I touched my finger to the middle license. "Dan Matthews."

Stan peered closer. "Could be him."

"It's him. And if this is his home address, that's about fifteen miles from here."

"You think he tried to go home?" Nash asked.

"I do. I think we should get that squad car at the station," I said. "And head that way, calling out a meeting place for him the entire way. If we find him great, if not, maybe he'll hear us."

"I'm game." Nash shrugged. "Stan, are you coming?"

"Yep. But one thing ..." Stan lifted his bottle as he stood up. "After that search ... we do the autopsy."

THIRTEEN
CALLING OUT

"Dan Matthews, if you are there," Nash spoke calmly over the speaker in the police car. "if anyone is out there, you are not alone. If you hear this. If you hear the sound of my voice. Please meet tomorrow at 1175 Grant Boulevard. We are survivors. We will meet you there."

He repeated the announcement over and over, almost robotically as we drove. Once in a while I took over, but for the most part it was Nash.

Stan decided to stay back and watch the cameras. He thought maybe he would spot something and to me that was a good idea.

We drove for a while, even making it to Dan Matthews' neighborhood. The way Nash repeatedly called out without emotion had me thinking of the movie, *I am Legend*, when I told Nash that, he said that in the original movie, *Last Man on Earth*, Vincent Price had done the same.

It was our idle conversation, nothing more, nothing deep and certainly nothing we'd talk about all over again with Stan.

It got to the point on the way back that we grew silent. Both in our own thoughts. I imagined Nash thought a lot about his family, he had lost so much.

Me, I kept thinking back to my fate. My punishment for taking a life, and somehow, being a survivor was in some way a form of punishment. I would have to live the rest of my life without atoning, and without forgiveness. All of Stephanie's family took their last breath absolutely hating me and there was nothing I could do.

Then again, who was I to even think about that when Nash and Stan lost all that they had.

"Bone saw," Nash popped out the words.

"I'm sorry. What?" At first I thought he was making some weird Star Trek reference about Bones.

"A bone saw," he clarified. "We need a bone saw."

"Okay, why?"

"For autopsy."

"Oh my God," I exclaimed. "I really don't want to do it. Why don't you do it?"

"I will if I have to. But it has to be done," Nash said. "I want to know what killed my family."

"Nash, we may never know," I said. "None of us are medical experts to the point we know by looking at a body, how he or she died."

"I know. But we have to try."

"You're right. We do."

"Don't you want to know?" he asked. "I mean, you don't seem like you want to know."

"Not really," I replied. "I don't see the point. It won't change anything. The only thing I want to know is why we died to survive, and this Dan Matthews didn't. If he didn't, others didn't."

"In theory, you're right." Nash nodded. "But where are they?

<><><><>

"Didn't spot a damn person," Stan said, still staring at the monitors when we returned. "Any luck?"

I shook my head. "No, not at all and Nash called out. By the way he said he would do the autopsy."

"I didn't."

"You did."

"No," Nash argued. "I said if there was no other way."

"Both work together," Stan suggested. "Speaking of which, I found a great place to do it." Stan placed his hands on the keyboard and typed slowly. "I think, yes." A hard click and monitor four changed to a building.

"An animal hospital?" I asked.

"Yep." Stan nodded. "An emergency animal hospital."

"We still need a bone saw," Nash said. "Have to cut the sternum and skull."

I glanced over to him. "You already know more than me."

"That's CSI and Autopsy Files on Netflix," Nash said.

"Oh, I love that show," Stan added.

I shook my head and my eyes cast upon the monitors. "Where's the hospital at?"

"Not far from Bethe's," Stan replied.

"Okay, yeah, I know where that is," I said. "It's on..." I paused when I saw it. Parked in the middle of a traffic jam, the backend smashed was a rust colored VW. There weren't many and it stood out. "Monitor Six. Where is that."

"The West End, right before the bridge, it's a 511 camera," Stan said.

"What's a 511 camera?" I asked. "Like an emergency?"

Nash explained. "It's the national camera system of the traffic and road information system. You could go on the website of any state and look of the major roads and cameras."

"And they tap in here," Stan said. "Lots of angles, see down the bottom. 511. Why?"

"Can you zoom in?" I asked.

Stan scoffed. "No, we can't zoom in. This isn't television."

"Actually." Nash reached down to the keyboard. "You can. Do you mind Stan?"

Stan rolled his chair out of the way. "Be my guest."

"What are we zooming in on?" Nash asked, poised and ready to handle my request.

"That rust colored VW," I said with a point. "Right there. See if there a Community College Sticker on the front. She worked there."

"Who?" Nash asked.

"My ex-husband's girlfriend."

"I can do you one better. The back end is smashed but I can still see … yep. There." Nash zoomed in to the license plate. Once it came into view he moved to the next computer and typed in. "Renee Arnold?"

"Oh my God, that is her car. She must not have been home when she sent that text."

Nash looked at me curiously.

"Long story but she said she was on her way to my house. She sent a text to my ex."

"Back up that camera get the whole car," Stan said. "I thought I saw something. Just a little."

Nash backed up the zoom making it wide.

Stan snapped his finger. "I did. That door is partially open."

I tilted my head and looked. "Yeah, but it was T-boned so maybe."

"No, there's no body in that driver's seat," Stan said.

"What?" I blurted out, shocked.

Nash brought in the camera closer. "I don't see a body either."

"Could she have fallen sideways from the impact?" I asked.

"Possible," Stan said. "But it's also possible, she's out there … alive."

FOURTEEN
IN SEARCH OF PAST

In all the apocalypse, dystopian, empty earth movies I have ever seen, there always seemed to be a mass sea of cars, jammed together from a worthless exodus. In the movies, some cars had people, some did not.

It made sense if people were trying to leave the city, but what hit us hit without warning and on a Sunday night. There were minimal cars in our neighborhood, traffic was light around the public safety building. All typical for a Sunday night. So why was Renee's car stuck in some traffic jam on the West End of town?

We were on the other side of the river and drove as close as we could to the bridge where I had seen Renee's car.

A flipped tractor trailer blocked the entire road, leaving me and Nash to walk the rest of the way.

Beyond that truck weren't too many vehicles until we reached the bridge.

"It's getting late," Nash said.

"I know."

"We can't look for too long. It's just not safe in the dark to walk."

"I know," I repeated. And it wasn't because of monsters of bad people, there was just so much carnage on the ground, it was a minefield of danger.

It was a wreckage nightmare on that bridge. Why were there so many cars? Walking through the stench of the decomposing bodies carried my way, it seemed to get worse every hour.

I tried not to look in the cars but was hard not to.

The faces of those who die, the last expression they made was agony. Whatever hit them, even though they died fast, those final moments were torture.

Again, it was another scene of sudden death meets car crash. Bodies were on the bridge, smashed between cars, on the hoods. It was horrible.

I imagined if those in the future would find the ruins or remains of our city. If they'd see the bridge and possibly skeletons if they remained.

A graveyard of people who were snatched from life instantly, just like in Pompeii.

Halfway across the bridge, I saw a woman. Her body lay horizontally across the hood of a blue sedan. Her face held that same agonizing expression and there was a massive slash down her face.

Not a lot of blood though. Her body told me why there was so much traffic,

She sported a tee shirt with a guitar graphic and the name Bane Stone.

A concert, they were all coming from a concert. The time made sense.

Renee was a huge fan of Bane Stone. That's where she was when she sent the text. Sitting in traffic.

It was tragic to think all those people were smiling, laughing, cheering and dancing not long before they met their demise.

At least their last memories were good.

I turned from the woman on the hood, took a few steps and froze, when I saw Nash step nonchalantly over the body of a woman. As if she weren't there or just a stone or fallen limb.

He kept walking.

I couldn't. I just couldn't move when I saw her. I didn't know the young woman but the pose of body, the twisted legs, head to the side and brown hair dangling across her face was all too familiar.

Seeing her instantly flashed me back to Stephanie.

To that day…

"911. What is your emergency?" the operator asked.

"I just killed someone."

"I'm sorry, Ma'am, did you just say you killed someone?"

With shivering breath, heart racing out of control, I nodded before verbally answering, "Yes" Shaking, I opened my car door, phone wedged between my shoulder and ear. I attempted to get out but realized I was still buckled in.

"Ma'am, where are you right."

"West Lincoln Street. Beaumont." My words trailed when I saw the people gather around the young woman on the ground. She was far enough away from my back end that I saw her in the rear view mirror, she had been thrown that far.

"Ma'am do you have an address?" the male operator asked.

There was another car a few feet from Stephanie and the crowd really started to gather. Some people cried out. There was so much shouting.

"Did someone call 911?" a person shouted.

"I'm on with them now," was a response from someone else.

"Ma'am?" the operator was in my ear.

"Is she alive," another person shouted.

"Oh my God, that's Stephanie Miller. Her poor mother."

"Ma'am."

"Somebody help her!"

"Ma'am."

Granted I was in a state of shock, but I was truly useless and standing there while strangers gathered to help. When I should have been the one. I was the guilty party. I slid the phone from my ear, and it dropped to the ground as I made my way over. My insides churning. It just seemed surreal.

Crouched by her was a man, he aided her. He looked like a construction worker or something.

He was younger than me and looked up to me. "Were you driving that car?"

I didn't answer.

"Were you? Did you call for help? She needs help."

He was by her head, his hand by her neck. I thought he was checking her pulse then I saw the blood puling through his fingers., He was trying to put pressure on a wound.

My whole body shuddered. Stephanie twitched; I'd never seen someone do that. She twitched her eyes wide open, hair dangling across her face.

Did she feel anything?

I did that. I did that to her. She was dying right there on the street, taking her last breath, totally helpless. I should have said

69

something. At the very least, I should have said I was sorry, to let her hear that I truly was, and always would be. But nothing. No words emerged.

She died in front of me, and I said nothing.

"Viv. Viv."

The sound of Nash's voice snapped me out of it.

"Is that her?" Nash asked.

"What?"

"Your friend," he said. "Is that her? You're looking at her like you know her."

"Um … no, it's not her. I don't know her … she looks familiar."

Nash nodded. "Come on, the car is not far ahead."

I took one more look at the woman and followed, but I was still stuck in the moment, stuck in the feeling of that day.

The sadness, the sickening feeling. Those moments after the accident that spoke volumes about my character. Things I didn't think of until they all said at the trial, that I showed no remorse or did anything to help.

Actions spoke louder than words, but I should have said the words to that poor girl.

Carrying that feeling across the bridge, I saw Nash by the rust colored VW. He stood on the passenger's side. I saw the look on his face. Something was wrong.

"What is it?"

"There's a body in there. We didn't see it on camera because…" He looked down to the passenger window.

I joined him. The head rested against the cracked passenger window facing down, her blonde hair was mangled, her body was in a half sitting position, parallel with the dashboard, her back was raised, and her feet were on the empty driver's seat.

"She could have been thrown from the driver's seat when she was T boned," Nash said. "I'm sorry."

"Me, too. But that's not her."

"What do you mean?" Nash asked.

"Renee has brown hair and is on the curvy side. This is her sister, Tina, I'm sure."

"Holy shit. So, she has to be alive."

I glanced back to the car; the windshield was intact. Renee wasn't thrown, she was gone, and the only explanation was she got out of the car and walked.

She was somewhere and if she was still alive. We had to find her.

FIFTEEN
NIGHT AGAIN

No one. Absolutely no one showed up. In city empty and silent, where a single noise travels the distance, bouncing off concrete ... no one came.

We stayed at the Safety building because it still had electricity and if it went off there were generators.

We wanted to keep an eye out on the cameras for specks of light and life. There were so many workers in that building at one time, the employee lounge was bigger than the first floor of my house.

While Nash and Stan settled, I left the building and walked next door to a place called Angel's Diner. They still had power as well and I made supper for everyone. In the freezer they had a tray of macaroni and cheese, while that cooked I fried up burgers. Figuring the produce and everything else wouldn't last, I gathered them along with that triple layer chocolate cake, loaded it on a busboy cart with wheels and headed back to the buildings. They knew I was cooking so I didn't worry about them eating.

They could hear me coming miles away, the cart rattled, and the silverware and planks clanked with every bump.

When I arrived in the monitoring room, Nash was staring at the screens and Stan was doing this swirling back and forth with his chair.

"Well, look at this," Stan said. "Smells great."

"You're welcome. But don't get me too much credit, they had a lot prepped and in the freezer." I began to unpack everything and put it on the table across the room.

Nash turned his chair and watched me make a plate. "This is really nice of you. Thank you."

"If you eat all your dinner, we have chocolate cake."

Stan clapped his hands together once. "Hot dog, cake and coffee sound great. But I am not touching that coffee machine." He tossed a glance Nash's way. "It's staring at me, saying brew me, brew me, but I keep thinking about Nash getting electrocuted. I won't pop back that easy."

"You'll be fine." I handed Stan plate. "I'll make you a cup to go with your cake."

"This looks really good, Viv, thank you." Stan stood.

"Where are you going?" I asked. "Aren't you eating with us?"

"I'm working on something up in the lounge, want to work a little more before I get tired," Stan replied. "I'll come back for the cake."

"I'll bring you a slice when I come up to make the coffee."

"Sounds like a plan." Stan with his plate, left the room and I fixed up a helping for Nash.

"I can make my own plate," Nash said. "You don't have to wait on me."

"What else am I going to do?" I handed him his supper then began to make mine. When I had my plate, I sat down next to him and noticed he hadn't touched his food. "What's wrong. You're not hungry."

"Oh, no, I'm starving. I was waiting for you," Nash said.

"That's really polite."

"Well." Nash shrugged. "I'm not that polite, my wife beat it in my head. It was a rule, I wasn't a lowed to eat until she sat down with hers. Mainly because I was always finished by the time she got the kids situated, fed and meat cut."

"Bet you ended up helping with those kids' plates."

"I did."

"Eat." I lifted my burger.

Nash brought his burger to his mouth, paused and stared at it. "Can I ask you something."

"Sure."

"What did you do with your husband's body? Not to be an appetite buster."

"I ... it's ... he's still in the kitchen. Why?" I asked.

"I buried my family in the yard. I was feeling guilty for doing that. Like I didn't wait or something." —"

"That's ridiculous. It's also amazing that you had that strength. It had to be hard to do."

Nash nodded. "It was. But I couldn't just leave them in their beds ... rot ... No, not that, I hate that word. Just say, I couldn't leave them there."

"I wish I had thought about burying Louis. I didn't because I didn't think it was real."

"Do you want to?" Nash asked.

"I do."

"Then before we leave the city, we'll do that. We have to leave the city, it's not gonna be good here. The smell alone."

"I know." Despite the conversation, I still ate my food.

"We'll bury him," Nash said. "I'd offer to bury Stan's family, but he's not wanting to admit their deaths."

"If he didn't see them, it's not real," I told him. "I envy that. But he knows everyone else is. He never had that moment of denial."

"I did. I thought I had died and was in some sort of purgatory."

"Me, too," I said. "Or hallucinating."

"How did you die?" Nash asked. "I mean if you don't want to tell me …"

"No, it's fine. Overdose. Various pills and vodka."

Nash stared at me. "That was intentional then."

"Very much so. After I took them, I sent Louis a text to pretty much say I did it. He came over, tried to save me. I guess he did."

"Can I ask you another question. A personal one?"

I nodded.

"Why?" Nash asked. "And don't take this the wrong way. Was it because you didn't want to go to jail?"

My heart instantly sunk to my stomach.

"I'm sorry," he said.

"No. No, I …I didn't know you knew who I was."

"I do. Not because I followed the story much," Nash said. "But because I was the 911 operator that took that call."

If my heart hadn't left my stomach it made its way there again.

"It's okay." Nash reached out and grabbed my hand. "I didn't testify because you pled guilty."

"I did it because I couldn't live with what I did. Then when they all got up and gave testimony, I just realized that the pain and guilt over what I did was far too much to bear. I know, I was taking the easy way out. When Stephanie's mother said she wished I had died, I did too. Now, please, I'm not saying this to get sympathy."

"Suicide is never the easy way out. It takes a lot of courage to take your own life," Nash said. "It wouldn't have resolved anything for them."

"And now living resolves nothing for me. I can't apologize again; I can't make it up to them and I'll never be able to forgive myself because her family died unable to forgive me."

"You don't know that," Nash said. "Maybe one of them forgave you."

"I'll never know, will I?"

"I'm sorry, Vivian, I shouldn't have brought it up. But if we're all going to be living together for a long time, I wanted you to know I knew, and I'll listen and talk to you any time. You hear? Anytime. I don't judge."

"Thank you."

"Can I offer you some advice?"

"Sure." I shrugged.

"Talk about it. It's gonna haunt you, no doubt, but you need to release your demons. The world went to shit when you took your last breath over an accident. You're alive for a reason."

"To continue to suffer," I said.

"Or find closure."

I wanted to tell him, 'Yeah, right like that will happen'. I wanted to throw back at him would he ever find closure for his losses. I was hurt that he brought it up, a bit bitter, but in a way I understood.

He was part of that tragic day.

It was a small world.

A small, dead, empty world and I hated living in it.

SIXTEEN
SMIDGEON OF HOPE

I could smell the coffee before I hit the employee break room. A fresh, good smell cutting through the stench of decay.

The door was closed, and I saw through the hallway window that Stan was seated at the table. Balancing the plate of cake, I opened the door.

When he had told me earlier he was working on something, I didn't think too much about it. Perhaps it was a puzzle, but that wasn't the case. He had various items spread out on the table, pen in hand, he'd lift his coffee to his lips, sip it and write.

"Did you bring my cake?" he asked, not looking up.

"I did."

"Thank you."

I found an empty spot at the edge of the table and set down the cake.

He lowered his pink cheaters to the end of his nose, then looked up at me. "Are you alright? You look like you've been crying."

"Just tired. Can I get you more coffee?"

"No, I'm good. Get some, might give you some energy."

It wasn't a bad idea, mugs sat next to the machine and poured a cup. 'This isn't the one that electrocuted him is it?"

"No, I got that from Maxwell's office," Stan replied.

"I didn't know you knew anyone."

"I didn't. I do now. Maxwell." After scanning the table, Stan lifted a business card and a small five by seven frame. He showed me the photo. It was one of a middle-aged man and woman taken in a Walmart portrait studio style setting. "Regional Director. He had a corner office, so I knew he was a big deal."

I reached for the chair next to Stan, but it was occupied by an open and empty gym bag, so I grabbed the next one and pulled it out. When I sat, I finally looked at everything on the table. Items that he must have pulled from that gym bag.

Pictures, brochures, business cards, licenses, name tags, and lots of phones.

Even though he wrote in the notebook, he was making notes on the cards and brochures.

When I watched him, I noticed the TS letters on the side of his pink readers. "TS?" I asked. "Those aren't your glasses?"

"Do I look like I would go by fancy pink frames?"

"Well …"

"No, I'm a dollar store guy. I got this from Trudy Smith. She worked at the bookstore on fifth. Hate to take from the dead, but they were so nice, and I couldn't see what books I was grabbing."

"They have cheaters at the bookstore. A rack right by the register," I said.

"Well, I didn't see that until I got Trudy's glasses. Terrible catch twenty-two."

"Did you know Trudy?"

"Nope."

Somehow that didn't surprise me.

He shuffled through the pile on the table and lifted a lanyard with the name tag and picture of Trudy Smith.

"Stan? What is all this?" I asked. "You have all these random things."

"Oh, they aren't random. Every single item here is from someone that in their own way, after death, has helped me since I got off that table at the hospital." Stan set down the name tag. "Trudy gave me the glasses." He pulled a cell phone. "This is Aisha's. She had four kids. I think four kids or a lot of nieces and nephews. She was at the hospital. First phone I took. She helped me to realize something happened to the world. Mark's phone." He lifted another. "He's had this phone for five years. Five years and the first picture he took was of his newborn son. You can go through every photo and watch his child grow." Stan shook his head with a smile. "Mark was the valet at the hospital, he gave me the blanket from the booth because I was cold. None of these people know what they did for me. But I did." He lifted the notebook. "I may not recall next week all the details, that's why I am writing them down."

"All these items, all of them are from people along the way."

"And each has a story. In here." He patted the notebook.

"I'd like to read it."

"Any time. It's not done. I don't suppose it will be done ever. Until I die. Unless you take up the mantra."

"I may do that for you," I said.

"It's not just for me. It's for anyone, now or in the future who finds this notebook."

"Why?" I asked. "Why for everyone. Isn't it mainly so you don't forget?"

"Oh, no. All these folks were people that loved and were loved. Had lives and did good things. They represent life. Humanity. If we don't right now, find a way to have them remembered," Stan said. "No one else will."

SEVENTEEN
IDLE IDOL

I held it in my hand, staring at it.

"My wife uses something that looks like that," Stan said. "For her feet."

"Electric foot file," Nash added.

"That's it." Stan snapped his finger. "Smooths out the heels. Looks like a handheld screwdriver."

I raised my eyes from the object. I was in shock, they discussed it like it was an item on eBay.

"Does it work?" Stan asked.

"Yeah," Nash replied. "I mean it turns on and spins, but I guess it's sharp. We'll find out."

Stan whistled. "It looks like it would make things easy. Wish I had that on Thanksgiving to get the damn legs off the bird without ripping the meat."

"Stop. Wait." I held up the object. "Where did you get this from?"

"Oh. The morgue," Nash replied. "It's an autopsy saw. Where else would I get it from."

"You got this from the morgue. When?" I questioned.

"This morning," Nash replied. "I wasn't in a good head-space. Not at all and I went out walking and didn't realize how close the morgue was to here. I went in."

"And why are we bringing this back here?" I asked. "Not doing the autopsy there."

"Look at you," Stan said. "All ready and willing to do this."

"I'm not. But it would make sense to do it in a morgue."

"It's not," Nash shook his head. "Trust me. It's not. Aside from there not being power, it's bad. I thought about Hassleman's Funeral home two blocks over, but it is locked up tight. So, the animal hospital is our best bet."

I cringed. "I'm not so sure I want to go there either. I love animals, I just ... it's not something I want to see."

"I understand," Nash said.

"If I may." Stan lifted his hand. "We can break into that funeral home. That's actually a better idea than the animal hospital. I mean, we're not finding any recently deceased there. And there aren't cops to arrest us."

"I'd rather do that." I examined the tool. "Not that I even know where to begin."

"That's why I got the book," Stan said. "Bottom line, it's now or never on doing the autopsy. Pretty soon the bodies will be too bad to dig into, the city is already smelling bad. We need to leave for our own good. But I don't want to leave without trying to find the answers."

We would take the car, since we did have a straight and easy shot to the funeral home. After cleaning off his desk, and sadly grabbing every picture he had on his corkboard, Nash grabbed the ax from the case in the stairwell, Stan took snacks from the breakroom, and we made our way out of the building.

It was the last time we'd be in there and I wasn't even thinking about the amount of time we spent riding around in the car, yelling out for survivors.

None of us did.

Until we saw the man sitting on the top step to the building, his back to us.

"Shoot," Stan said in a whisper. "We almost didn't leave a note. If he wasn't there ..."

The man turned around, almost startled and jumped up.

We probably looked like quite the trio standing there just as stunned to see him.

Maybe even dangerous. Nash with the Ax, me holding that autopsy saw.

He was a middle aged man, dressed in jeans, a tee shirt and a purple dress shirt that was open.

"Holy cow, you're here," he said. "I heard the announcing. It was in the distance and there wasn't a note like the guys said .... I figured I'd wait. I almost left. Good thing I didn't. Holy cow, I can't believe you're here."

"Holy cow," I said. "You're Bane Stone."

"Who?" Stan asked.

"Bane Stone," I explained. "He's a musician. He's been a round for a long time."

Nash added. "He was doing a concert here Sunday night."

"Bane Stone?" Stan questioned. "What kind of name is Bane."

"Not my real one, sir." He extended his hand. "My real name is Nick."

"I like that better. I'm calling you Nick." Stan shook his hand.

"Everyone that knows me does."

I couldn't believe it. More than an aging singer, it was another survivor. "Are you alone?" I asked. "Of course, you are, sorry."

"No." He shook his head. "I'm not alone. Yesterday when I was trying to track where your message was coming from, which direction, I ran into someone. Just like me, chasing the PA voice. Apparently we were like blocks away from each other for the whole day. Strange, both of us just stunned and in disbelief."

"Where is he now?" Stan asked.

"Oh, it's a she," Nick answered. "She's a couple miles from here. We buried her boyfriend last night and now she's looking for his ex-wife, she thinks she ..."

The rest of his words were a blur, drowned out by my heart that beat out of control. "She is," I blurted out. "I think. Is the woman you're with Renee?"

He stuttered his response. "Yeah ... yeah she is."

I actually smiled. I smiled and gasped out.

I felt overwhelmed and overjoyed. Not only would we find Renee, but maybe some answers as to how she survived without dying.

EIGHTEEN
CONNECT

The drive back to Beaumont seemed like it took an eternity, even though we had a clear shot going there and in reality didn't take long at all. Nick's description of where Renee said she was headed was off, mainly because he didn't know the area. I couldn't even guess.

"She wanted to check the ambulances," Nick told us. "We saw several on the way to find her boyfriend. They had crashed but we saw them."

"Ambulances?" Nash asked.

Nick nodded. "When we got to the house and saw the woman - you," he looked at me. "Wasn't there and the dried vomit and pills, she assumed the ambulance had come and taken you. Her boyfriend was calling for help."

That was when it hit me. I had cut him off when we met. I never got to hear him finish his sentence about why Renee was looking for me. "Wait. She's looking for me not because she thinks I'm alive?" I asked.

"She's looking," Nick replied. "So, she can bury you."

Stan blurted out a whispering, "Jesus."

Nash whistled. "Won't she be in for a surprise."

"She'll be happy though," I said. "Even though she is my ex-husband's girlfriend, she'll be happy, she was always nice and supportive to me."

I was excited to find her.

We started at my house and four blocks away, not far from her home with Louis. I spotted her walking. A green blanket draped over her shoulders. I wasn't even sure she needed a blanket, the weather was mild.

Maybe it was a security thing, I didn't know. But when Stan commented about the blanket, Nick replied that Renee was saying she was cold and couldn't warm up.

To me that meant emotions.

She buried the man she loved and was searching for his ex-wife.

We stopped the car as soon as we turned the corner. I was the only one that stepped out, at least at first.

"Renee," I called to her.

She stopped, her back remaining to me.

"Renee," I called again, moving hurriedly her way.

Slowly, she peered over her shoulder. Her brown hair danced into her eyes. If I were to read the expression on her face, it looked as if she were in shock to see me.

Of course, she was in shock. She thought I was dead, she was looking for my body.

Why would she even suspect I was alive? The last she knew I OD'd.

I didn't call her name again, I didn't need to. She saw me and finished turning around.

Renee said nothing. The blanket slipped from her shoulders to the sidewalk as she staggered to me.

I realized seeing me was probably a bit much.

She was more overwhelmed than me I supposed.

I heard the shutting the of the car doors as we neared each other.

At that moment I was waiting for her excitement, her happiness to see me alive.

As she stepped closer to me and I to her, I anticipated her embrace. Her grateful arms around me. I expected that.

What I didn't expect was the moment she was close enough, Renee, without saying a word ... decked me.

"Here." Stan handed me the white square object. "It's one of those shake and twist cold packs. That will help with the shiner you're gonna have."

"Where dd you get it?"

"Walgreens."

We had returned to the house on Murkin and Price, not only because it was close, but because it was one we were certain had supplies and no dead bodies.

"How's it feel?" Stan asked.

"Hurts. Not as much as my feelings are hurt. But, then again, par for the course." I put the pack to my eye and winced.

"Any idea why she'd hit you?" Stan asked.

"I thought she liked me."

"Maybe she never did."

I grumbled.

"She was looking to bury you. Maybe it was a good riddance sort of thing."

"Thanks."

"In all seriousness, I asked her. I asked her why she hit you," Stan said. "She said, 'go away old man.'"

"Oh my god, that's horrible and doesn't sound like her."

"She didn't say that."

"I thought you said in 'all seriousness' didn't you?"

"I did. She didn't answer when I asked. I think she's waiting on you to ask."

"Where is she?" I questioned.

"In the den sipping on the brandy."

I turned my head curiously at him.

"Yeah, I know, right? I thought only people in New Hampshire drank brandy."

"Do you think it's safe to talk to her?" I asked.

"Meaning, do I think she'll beat you up again?" Stan shrugged. "Don't know. But you're tough. You can take it. Plus, this time you'll see it coming."

I stood from the kitchen chair and handed him the pack. "I'll be back. Hold that for me."

"You should be holding that on your eye. First hour is crucial."

"I'll be fine."

I made my way to the den. I knew where it was. It was in the front of the house, across the foyer from the living room. When I arrived at the open door, I saw Renee sitting on the window seat staring out, much like I did when I saw Nash on that stormy night.

"Can we talk without violence?" I asked.

She looked at me then back to the window.

"Everyone is dead, Renee. I am so happy to see you alive. I thought... I thought we were sort of friends."

Renee chuckled as she kept her gaze out that window. "You thought I was your friend. Friends don't pull the shit you did."

"What ... do you mean?"

"You did it, Viv. You did it. You fucking downed a bottle of pills with a vodka chaser. Do you know how that made me feel?" Renee asked harsh, finally looking at me. "I heard the desperation in Lou's voice. He was destroyed. We cared, Viv. We cared so much about you. We were there for you and would be every step of the way."

"I know that. You just don't understand what I was going through. Why I did it."

"I don't care. When he sent that text about you, I flew out of that concert, noise blockers still in my ears, and even with them I could still hear him screaming on the phone." She closed her eyes.

"I'm sorry. But if you were that upset, why ...why did you hit me?"

"I'm angry at you." She clenched her fist. "I am so angry at you. I really don't want to look at you."

Her words burned and I felt them. Like some desperate child looking for approval, I asked, "Why?"

"You wanted to die. You tried to die. Louis went over there, and he fucking saved you. He's in the ground. And you, the person who didn't want to live is still here. My mother, sister, father, everyone that wanted to live ... is gone. But Vivian ... is still here. So, I don't really care if you are a survivor of this — whatever happened. Guess what Viv, in my heart you got your wish. You're dead to me," she said. "And you always will be."

A year ago, before the Stephanie death, I would have taken her words of ones spewed forth in grief, but there in then I took them to heart.

A buried hatred for me emerged and I deserved everything she said.

I believed I deserved what she said. What she implied.

In so many words she was saying I was unworthy perhaps even a coward.

That's what I heard.

Sticks and stones may break my bones, but names will never hurt me.

Wrong.

Whoever said that was completely wrong,

Words stung more than the punch to the eye.

For a brief blip in time, I had been given a slight reprieve of my pain and guilt, believing living was my punishment.

I was wrong.

My punishment was not only living with the guilt, living when everyone else died, but also living with someone who would constantly remind me of the simple truth.

I didn't deserve to be alive.

NINETEEN
DIGGING IN

I made the decision to stop trying with Renee. I had given it a few more tries over the hour before we headed to the funeral home, but that was it.

She was angry and mad, and I punished myself enough as it was. Allowing her to add to that was completely masochistic.

Life was hard enough with all that was going on. Having her declare how mad she was that I didn't die, was just ludicrous.

Or maybe it wasn't.

At that point in time, I was so let down because I was so happy she was alive, I guess I expected the same.

It was a hard pass for both Rene and Nick on doing the autopsy. In fact, Renee was pretty hardcore against it. Nick did offer to help Nash get a body and said he knew where to get a decent one.

Whatever that meant.

After breaking the front window of the Funeral Home, Nash climbed inside, opened the door and left Stan and I to get things ready while they retrieved a body.

We found the preparation room or embalming room in the rear of the building. I thought it would be in the basement, but it wasn't. It was behind two large heavy doors and down a hall.

We left those doors propped open so Nash and Nick could find us.

Admittedly, the funeral home was the only place that truly felt normal. No bad smells. Nothing.

The stainless steel table was clean, and Stan was excited. In fact, he did a little skip when he found a drawer full of tools. "Look at this," he said then whistled. "Most of these are in the book."

And he had that book all ready. When he claimed he was going to read it to me, I thought he was joking. I had looked through it, but it was like reading IKEA furniture instructions without the furniture to reference.

We waited a while for them to return. I didn't understand what was taking them so long, there were literally bodies everywhere.

"How about this," Stan said. "Vicks." He placed the large jar on the counter. "It will help with the smell."

Oh, God, the smell. I didn't look forward to that.

I prepared to apply a generous amount under my nose when I heard Nash's voice in the distance.

"I don't understand," Nash spoke in a complaining manner. "Not only did we get the heaviest body, but we had to carry him four blocks."

"It's no where near as bad as the others," Nick replied.

"He smells."

"Not as bad as others."

"Oh, God, my fingers just sunk in his legs. "

"That's because that was the only part not in the freezer."

"And I have that end."

"You asked."

Stan looked at me. "Oh, boy."

We heard the arguing voices draw closer.

Thumping and grunting precluded their arrival. I could smell the body before they entered the room.

They carried a large man, I wouldn't say fat, he was just big, and with a counting, 'one, two, three', they hoisted him on the table.

When he plopped down it was like a sack of flour, but instead of white dust billowing out it pelted out a cloud of odor.

"Okay, I'm done. I'm out," Nick said. "Good luck."

Stan, with that book walked closer to the table. "He's in good shape." He spoke of the body.

I nodded as I looked at him. "All except his feet."

The poor man's feet had decomposed to the point they oozed through his shoes.

"Look at you," Stan said, "You're already doing page one." He turned to Nash. "Where did you get him?"

"Door Stop Diner," Nash replied. "He was pretty much in the freezer, except, well, his feet. Must have fell that way."

Stan peered over his glasses, "I don't see a name tag. Did you check the pockets? You know I like to know who is helping us out."

"Yep, I did. No phone, but …" Nash reached behind him and then extended a wallet to Stan. "Found that."

"Good boy."

I stared down to the man. His face was gray and purple, his skin hadn't rotted yet, but it was tight. He had a mustache and a thick head of hair. He had to be around six and a half feet, he extended almost the length of the table.

He still had on his clothing. Chef's clothing, he probably was a cook at that diner, closing for the night.

"Guys, if I'm doing this, you undress him."

"Hot dog, you memorized the book." Stan said, staring in the wallet. "Let's thank Bill Berryman and get started."

TWENTY
WHAT'S ON YOUR MIND

The autopsy saw vibrated in my hand when I turned it on to test it. I imagined the vibration would be worse once it touched the body.

I hated what I was about to do and had to put myself in some strange mindset, as if playing a gross adult version of the game Operation.

Grabbing a mortician's apron and protective covering, I positioned myself at the side of the table. The face shield helped a little with the smell and didn't hinder my vision.

"Let's do this," I said. "Stan."

"Page one," he read. "*With patient in a supine position ...* oh, how cute, it says in parenthesis 'on their back'," he continued. "*With patient in a supine position. Begin visual examination. Make notations of any visual irregularities such as bruises, scrapes, puncture or gun shot wounds.* Hmm, it's nice to know a gunshot wound is an irregularity."

"I don't see any of those," I said.

"I'm pretty sure he wasn't shot or stabbed," Stan replied. "I think we can skip stage one."

"Okay yes." I nodded.

"*Bend elbow to check for Rigor Mortis.* Nah, you don't need to know when he died, we know that. Let's move on."

He flipped a page. "Here we go. Here's the good stuff. Grab the scalpel."

I lifted it.

"You may need to press hard on this," Stan said then read. *"Make a Y incision.* Like this ..." he held up the book and showed me. "See it goes arm to arm, to the breastbone and then to the penis. It doesn't say penis it says pubic bone."

"I get it."

"Go deep," Stan explained. "It has to cut through the abdomen wall so you can peel —"

"Alright I get it."

"Just reading the instructions."

My hand shook a little as I hovered the scalpel.

"Do you need a drink?" Stan asked.

"What? No? I'm nervous."

"Here," Nash said. "I'll do the cuts."

Exhaling, I handed him the scalpel. "Thank you."

After looking once more at the illustration, Nash began the incision. I don't know why I expected blood, but there was none, just a thick oozing of something dark and coagulated.

It looked tougher to cut than I thought, it was that moment when I really noticed the tattoo on Bill's right bicep. A fighter jet with the name 'Dad' on it.

That's when it hit me.

"Guys, if everyone dropped dead at once, why are there no planes crashed anywhere? Surely we would have seen or heard one crash."

Nash paused.

Stan peered up from the book. "You're right."

"Or birds," Nash added. "I didn't see any birds."

"Right? I mean we've seen every other domestic animal with humans. No birds, no planes. I didn't even think of it until I saw his ink," I said.

"I read a book once," Nash said. "About some event that happened, and the plane couldn't land because it was deadly, like methane on the ground. They had to keep flying."

Stan chuckled. "Oh, come on, that's the most ridiculous store line I ever heard. Like the movie Speed in the sky."

"Yes," Nash nodded. "I mean you had a level of suspension of disbelief …"

"Yeah, suspend disbelief until next Thursday," Stan scoffed. "Just cut the body."

"We need to head to the airport," I said. "We do. Before we leave town, we need to go there."

"As if all the planes that didn't crash decided to land?" Stan asked.

I nodded.

"Okay, that's a plan. I think we just didn't see any crashed planes because it was a Sunday night. They're out there. Once we get out of this town, we'll see them. Nash get to work."

"I'm on it." Nash lowered the scalpel.

When finished, he looked at me. "All you."

I shifted my eyes to Stan. "What's next?"

"Peel back the flaps," Stan answered. "The top flap goes over the face. Not sure why that's important. If he made the cut deep enough you should see the organs."

I peeled back the flaps, which did so relatively easy, despite feeling thick. But I didn't see organs, some intestines but that was it. "I am going to assume we need to cut the ribs?" I turned my head to the sound of the saw.

Nash held it.

I was so grateful that Nash took that on. It took several minutes, but he soon had the rib cage removed.

Stan turned the page. "*Remove all organs and put them on a table for examination.*"

I approached Bill and looked into his wide open body cavity. I could see every organ. "His lungs are good. Heart doesn't look enlarged." I reached down. "I'll know more when I remove it."

"Good girl," Stan said.

"Whoa, okay. Bill was a drinker. A heavy one." I reached for the liver and lifted it. "Wow. Look at this. All these abrasions and malformations. Definitely stage four cirrhosis. He wasn't healthy with this."

"How in the hell do you know that is stage four cirrhosis?" Stan asked.

"My father died of stage four cirrhosis," I replied.

"Again," Stan said. "How did you recognize that."

"My mom had the mortician take a polaroid of his liver and put it on the fridge so I would see it and never drink."

"Oh my God," Nash blurted. "Your mom put a polaroid of your dead dad's liver on the fridge."

"Yep." I nodded. "My mom was strange."

"Obviously, it didn't work," Stan said.

"Obviously." I continued removing the organs and didn't see anything, other than the liver that looked suspicious. Even with the slight decaying. "Nothing internally.:

Stan flipped a page. "Now for the brain. Make an incision in the back of the scalp from ear to ear. The lift the skin and peel over the face. Use a vibrating saw to cut the circumference of the skull and remove." He glanced at me. "Sounds easy."

"You aren't the one doing it," I said and grabbed the scalpel.

"Do you want me to?" Nash asked.

"I think I'm good now. I just removed every organ in Bill's body." I walked from the side of the table to the head and that was when I noticed it. His ears. A dried thick pink substance pooled in his ear canals, seeping out of his lobes.

Stan noticed my pause. "What is it Viv?"

"He has dried cerebral fluid in his ears." I turned his head it was the same on the other side. I didn't say anything, not at that moment, I needed to see.

Using the scalpel, I did exactly as Stan instructed. After pulling the skin over the face, I took the autopsy saw and carefully and slowly, cut a circumference around the skull.

Both hand on the bone, I gently pulled back expecting to see the brain.

Instead, the second I lifted the cap of the skull, this substance just seeped out. It was thick and gray. It was obviously at one point the brain, but it had fallen apart, destroyed as if Bill had acid injected into his head.

"That doesn't look right," Stan said.

"It's not," I replied. "I think we know what killed everyone."

Nash scratched his head. "How the hell does that happen to the brain. Apparently the brain is destroyed. That doesn't just happen in a second. Everyone's brain, at once. How?"

"I'm not an expert." Stan pointed his pen. "But those ears might be a clue."

"Okay. Again, how?" Nash repeated. "I mean what would do this?"

TWENTY-ONE
WITH PURPOSE

Without really knowing what made it happen, we knew the cause of death, at least for Bill it was the brain. The brain is the main hub, it went down, destroyed, so Bill went down.

But how?

I had never heard of a brain turning into just a mush substance.

We put Bill back together and covered him. On the way back to the house, I stopped at every body I saw. I looked at the ears. Sure, enough, like Bill, they had the pink pooling. It wasn't as deep or as dark as blood, so it wasn't noticeable at first.

Now it stood out to me.

Stan and Nash carried on a conversation regarding what we learned but my mind was busy thinking. I didn't engage with them, I was stuck on what I saw. It was so out there, that I didn't want to be the one to tell Nick and Renee, because it was unbelievable.

Their faces and expressions held so much disbelief.

What choice did they have but to accept what we said?

"Like gone?" Nick asked. "The brain was just gone?"

"It was there," I replied. "But it wasn't in a solid state."

"We can only conclude," Nash added. "The same happened to everyone."

Renee held her arms crossed tightly. "If it was that fast. Do you think these people felt anything? Pain? Thoughts? Emotions?"

I shook my head. "I think …"

Renee held up her hand. "I really don't want to hear from you."

Thinking, 'whatever', but not saying it, I turned away and let Nash answer.

"If it hit the brain and destroyed the brain that fast, no they felt nothing, then again we're not experts."

Nick asked. "How? How is this possible?"

Nash shook his head. "You two were alive when it happened. Us three were dead. Whatever it was didn't affect us maybe because our brain wasn't working properly at that second. But you guys, you have to be the key to us figuring out what happened. If we can figure out why you weren't hit, maybe we can figure out how it occurred."

"We'll never figure it out," Renee said. "None of us are scientists."

I wanted to say something but then again, I didn't want Renee to say once more she didn't want to hear from me.

Hear from me.

Replaying her striking words, caused my mind to replay other words she had said to me.

When he sent that text about you, Renee had said, I flew out of that concert, noise blockers still in my ears, and even with them I could still hear him screaming on the phone.

Hear.

Noise blockers.

Ignoring Renee, I faced Nick. "What were you doing when it happened. Did you see anyone go down?"

Nick shook his head. "No, I was in my trailer watching … Watching YouTube videos."

"Odd question," I said. "You weren't wearing headphones were you?"

"Earbuds, yes, why?"

"That's it," I said. "It has to be the delivery of it. The skull is a case that protects our brain. If we hurt our brain, say fractured skull and we have a cerebral bleed, there are two ways for fluid to escape. Our nose or ears. So that goes to figure there are two ways to affect the brain. Whatever caused this entered the bodies one of those two ways. But the common denominator with Renee and Nick is they both had their ears blocked."

Stan held up his hand. "Stop. You used the word 'delivered'?"

"Like a weapon?" asked Nash.

"It has to be," I said. "Mother nature just doesn't burb up some mystical fumes that melt a brain like the book you talked about."

"Is there anything even like this?" Nick questioned. "Who has this technology? Is it Aliens?"

Before I could reply, Stan did.

"Russians," Stan said.

Nash groaned. "That is always the answer from your generation. Blame the Russians."

"I'm not blaming the Russians," Stan said. "He asked who has this technology. I said the Russians because of the Havana Syndrome."

"I'm sorry, the what?" Nash asked.

"Havana Syndrome," Stan explained. "Back in 2016 hundreds of US diplomats and spies suffered from this syndrome. They swore they heard a buzzing, a pressure in their head. Not sure, but it affected their brain. Some say it was a weapon using microwaves. Some say it was the Russians. Whatever it was, it was real. This ... this sounds like of a stronger version of the Havana thing."

Hearing this stumbled me back. "You're totally serious. This is a real thing."

Stan nodded. "If we go to the library we can find books. This sounds like it."

"Still could be aliens," Nick stated. "Maybe they did the Havana Syndrome thing as a test. Saw it didn't cause people to die and upped their game."

"Whatever it is," Stan said. "I think Vivian is right. It's a weapon and that means one thing. If it's a weapon, unless it's aliens ..." he gave a nod to Nick. "People are alive and basically, one way or another, we are at war."

TWENTY-TWO
THE JOURNEY

Four days.

It had been four days and the world as I saw it was over.

It became the physical embodiment of the world I felt I lived in before everyone dropped dead.

Destitute, gray.

Now I saw it. Physically saw it.

The only difference was people talked to me. They spoke to me, other than Renee, without judging me for being a monster.

Nash was aware but he didn't judge.

I suspected by Renee's behavior she hated me long before my accident and put on a front for Louis because he wanted to be there for me.

Nick and Stan were clueless. One day I would tell them, at least Stan. I wasn't sure that Nick hadn't been informed by Renee. He didn't act it. Usually when people found out I killed a young woman with my car, they were standoffish, even if they didn't mean to be. Subconsciously they pulled back not wanting anything to do with a murderer.

Odd as it was, in a post-apocalyptic event world, for me it was much less lonely.

We spent that last night in the house on Murkin. No power, just candles and a cold supper.

We came up with a plan, at least for the immediate. We would go west, look for an isolated spot, away from the city and the mounds of bodies. A place that could give warmth in the winter and growth for food.

It would have to be near fresh water for fishing.

An older atlas gave us several choices to check out. We would do that. There were no massive amounts of survivors, so food in the stores was still plenty. We could stockpile for the fall and winter, setting our sights on planting for the next year.

Most of the bigger home stores had put out the seeds for spring planting, we marked those down as a must to get.

We had time to find the perfect place. There was no hurry.

Did we want to look for survivors? To me, it didn't matter either way. We never did find Dan Mathews, the young man that escaped out of Bethe's.

I really felt survivors were out there, but like Dan they wouldn't be easy to find.

Before we ventured off to find a place, we would go to the airport.

Satisfy my curiosity and theory.

I believed if the planes weren't affected they landed somewhere.

It did seem as if I was the only one who wanted to go, that the trip to the airport to the others was a bother.

They weren't happy, not when we decided on it at night and not in the morning when we woke up.

I heard the mumbling and attitude from Renee, even Nash thought it was a waste.

What difference did it make if we went to check it out? What hurry were we in?

The only hurry there happened to be, was getting out of the city.

It was time to go. The night was cool, so the windows remained closed, but the need to leave was reiterated when we stepped out the door.

The overwhelming stench of rotting bodies was everywhere.

It was in every breath I took.

We loaded in the SUV, all gassed up. How far that gas would take us, we didn't know or if we'd be able to get more gas.

Maybe that was what irked everyone. They thought we were detouring to the airport.

I didn't see it as a detour since we were already headed west, and the airport was seventeen miles that way.

We were just taking a different route.

Since everything happened on a Sunday night, the highway was clear. A few cars here and there that had veered off the road, some crashed into others, some went over the embankment. Nothing gave us concern or blocked our way. The entire drive, I kept an eye out for ways to go around should we hit some sort of blockade.

It was just after the 'Airport Three miles' sign that I knew something was wrong. I didn't say anything, but I saw things on the road that brought pause.

A piece of rubber.

Metal that looked like a sign but burnt.

Driving into the sun, made it hard to see what was ahead. About a mile or so before the airport was a small grade. It was as if the crest in the highway and the sun blocked it all for a big reveal.

As soon as we reached the top, we had no choice but to stop.

I had stated that I hadn't seen or heard a plane fall from the sky, that I didn't truly believe they did all fall. But I couldn't deny it any further when we saw the wreckage that not only sprawled across the four lanes of highway but created a crater that made it impossible for us to drive any farther.

"Well, I guess your theory was wrong," Stan said. "I'm sorry. I was hoping you were right."

Nash added. "It's possible she still may be right, maybe this plane was low enough to be affected. Crashing on its way to land."

I stepped out of the vehicle.

Across newspapers, the internet, I had seen pictures of airplane crashes, everyone had. But they were carefully edited or shot to avoid graphic images.

There was no filter on what was before me.

It was like a Lego airplane, dropped and smashed, some pieces were recognizable some just bits. Only a small fraction of the fuselage remained intact. I could see the bodies still in their seats. Others were strewn across the crater, most in pieces and naked. Scattered bits of white and colors speckled across the dirt and upturned pavement.

I wanted to vomit.

The only thing that made the scene tolerable was the fact that none of them knew what was happening.

Or maybe they did.

The others had joined me, standing on the edge of that crater staring down.

"I guess that's it," Stan said. "We turn around."

"Wait," Nash said abruptly, then spoke fast. "Wait. Wait. Wait."

I looked at him. "What do you see?"

"Not see—" he pointed up.

As soon as he did that, I heard.

At first it sounded like a rush of air, steady and in the distance. It grew louder, fuller. I turned back toward the sound which came from behind us and saw the white smoke.

The noise grew thunderous, vibrating. All of us gazed to the sky as three fighter jets roared not that high above us. Like they were doing an air show, they flew off, then within seconds, circled around and returned to fly over us again.

My heart sunk after, of course, it beat out of control. "Oh my God."

Renee screamed enthusiastically, as if it were some sort of rescue. Perhaps it was.

Everyone was excited and acting it except Nash. I noticed it and looked curiously at him.

"What is it?" I asked.

"You might want to curb your enthusiasm," he said. "They weren't ours."

TWENTY-THREE
HOLD ON

We were instantly a group of five divided. Stan in the middle like Switzerland, neutral in reaction, saying nothing after Nash made the announcement that the jets flying overhead were not American planes.

They made one more pass which allowed all of us to see them. How Nash determined they weren't American planes was beyond me. They went by so fast.

"We have to go," Renee said in a panicked voice. "We have to go."

"Go where?" I asked.

"You…" she pointed at me. "Brought us into this."

"Oh, so it's my fault foreign planes are flying overhead."

"Yes."

"Ladies," Stan said calmly. "Let's not argue. It's no one's fault we're at war. Well, at least no one right here. Obviously, we can't go forward." He glanced at me, then turned to Renee. "And we can't go back. If war planes are flying, the cities are not safe."

Nick let out a short groan. "I can't believe this. I can't. Someone deliberately did this to us? They wiped us out."

"It was bound to happen," Stan stated. "I mean, it's better than a nuke."

We all looked at him.

"It is." Stan shrugged. "At least the plants and ground are fine. Which ... is smart. Take over a country that isn't destroyed."

"If the cities aren't safe," Renee said. "Then what?"

"We don't know that the planes are part of some massive war movement," I said. "We don't. I mean, maybe they came to help."

"Stop it," Renee snapped.

"Be nice," Stan said calmly.

"We need to find a farm," Nick stated. "Or a really rural area."

"We're headed in the right direction," I said and turned. "What do you think?" That was when I noticed Nash wasn't there. "Where did Nash go?" I stepped from the group calling out, "Nash!"

The others called out as well.

I worried that he tripped and had fallen into the airplane wreckage, that he was hurt.

It was a strange world now, and one injury could mean death.

"Nash!" I hollered out.

"Here," he responded, his voice coming from the distance.

I pivoted my body toward the sound of his voice, he came from the treelined area on the west bound lane of the highway just off the wreckage.

"Here," Nash repeated then appeared. "I wanted to see something." He made his way back to the group. "The wreckage didn't take out the trees and I knew Anderson

Road ran parallel to this. It's fine. If we backtrack to the exit, we can take Anderson around this."

Renee asked. "And go where?"

"West," Nash replied. "Toward the airport."

"Seriously?" she said with a snippy tone. "We just saw the planes flying over us and you want to go to the airport to what? Greet the enemy."

"We don't know," Nash said. "We don't know anything."

Renee folded her arms and scoffed.

"If they invaded us," Nash said. "They aren't going to shoot us all. This isn't Red Dawn."

"Isn't what?" I asked.

"Red Dawn?" Nash repeated. "You don't know that movie."

Stan spoke up. "I'm surprised you do. I mean the original was a while ago and the reboot, well, no one remembers that."

"Anyhow ..." Nash continued. "It was about our country being invaded. Look. We can't just go run and hide, we need to find out what's going on."

"What do you propose?" Stan asked.

"I say we go forward," Nash said. "Go toward the airport, like we planned. If there is another country here whether invading or helping, that's where they are going to be. That has to be the hub."

Nick shook his head. "And you just want to drive up to the gate."

"You have a better idea?" Nash asked.

Renee nodded. "Yeah, go back, find some rural area. Lay low."

"Why don't we do this," Stan said. "Why don't we do both. We not put all the eggs in one basket. A couple of us stay back, find a place to lay low, find another vehicle, send the others out. Put a time frame up. Those who stay back, if they don't hear anything from the ones that went to the airport, they go looking for them. In fact," Stan snapped his finger, "we can hit that Walmart and grab some radios. They might still work."

"We're not far from Dodson," Nash said. "It's a bump in the road town. Those who hang back can hang back there."

"What do we think?" Stan asked. "We really do need to find out something. I mean a few days ago, I thought I was Charlton Heston and the lone survivor in the world. All of you did. We weren't and we're not alone. We just need to find out who is left."

I didn't hear any objections to Stan's idea. Everyone seemed to be in agreement, we also knew, without saying a word, who would go and who would stay behind in Dodson.

Nash and I would be airport bound.

TWENTY-FOUR
BEYOND THE ROAD

The town of Dodson was only a few miles from the highway. I didn't think the radios would work, but we picked them up anyhow with batteries, along with binoculars and a hunting rifle.

A small diner with four cars parked outside gave us the extra vehicle to leave behind for Stan, Renee and Nick. It was easy to find the keys. There were only a few diners in the place, and one man seated at the counter, his head smashed into his burger, had his keys setting right by his coffee.

No more planes flew by, the world returned to silence.

There was a certain look on Stan's face. Was it concern? Fear? Almost as if he didn't want to say anything. He had grabbed a small box of cereal. One of the individual ones from the diner and was eating from it like popcorn. Focused entirely too much on each piece he lifted from the box.

The plan was he, Renee and Nick would wait in the parking lot of the Motel Six while Nash and I headed toward the airport.

The Motel Six was Renee's idea, it set back off the road and was hidden.

The rooms had kitchens, not that it made a difference.

We were to head out, scout and return with intel. If within two hours they didn't hear from us, they were to come looking.

"That's not gonna happen," Stan said. "At least with them two," he spoke hushed. "I just think they aren't gonna come. Nick has the keys."

"Come with us," I told him.

Stan shook his head. "I want to but if they don't come for you, someone has to." He then lifted up a set of keys with a tiny rabbit dangling on them. "Got these from the cook. It's the blue van. I'm ready."

"We'll be back," I assured him.

"Two hours," Stan reiterated. "Clock starts ticking now."

After reiterating what we had planned to do to 'scope' the airport, I darted a kiss to Stan's cheek and left with Nash.

Anderson Road ran parallel with the highway, a half mile section of land separated them. Some spots had trees, some homes. Many times, driving on Anderson I could see the highway.

Even in Dodson, we weren't far from the airport. Getting to there from Anderson Road was easy. After the plane crash we could get back on the highway. But did we really want to drive through the front door?

While we hadn't seen the planes again, they had flown by and weren't a figment of our imagination. If Nash was correct and they weren't ours and by some chance they were an 'enemy' then it wasn't smart driving up to the departure entrance.

Years before there was a place called Woodlyn Drive-In Theater. It set on top of a hill that overlooked the airport.

It was there a long time and shut down shortly after they built the new airport. The land was used for a weekly Sunday flea market that attracted people from the tristate area.

I hadn't been to Woodlyn in decades, but somehow, even though it was a flea market, it still looked like a drive-in movie. The white posts that held speakers popped up like tombstones across the large gravel lot.

We parked at the front where the screen once perched and walked to the edge.

It was a great view. I could see for miles.

Sure enough, we could see movement at the airport. Planes packed the runways, trucks rolled by. I could see people walking, they wore combat style uniforms, dark in nature, almost black, but where they were from were hard to discern.

But there were people and a lot more than us four.

Like Nash, I peered through the binoculars.

"These are shit," Nash said. "I can't make anything out."

"Me either." The people were just slightly bigger dots.

"We need to figure out what's going on. Whether it's safe to approach, you know, like it's a rescue or an invasion."

When I lowered my binoculars, I watched Nash scan the area.

"We have to get closer." He pivoted to the right. "There." He pointed.

I didn't know what he was pointing at, I had to lift my binoculars again and the only thing I could figure he was indicating were the cargo hangers set far away from the airport.

"The UPS hanger is closest. It has that little grade with bushes. From there we should be able to get a good look and stay covered."

"Yeah, but how do we get there without going through the airport."

"Oh, there's a whole other entrance for the businesses. It's off Beaver Road. I don't see any guards or trucks." He lowered his binoculars. "What do you say? We drive close, lay low in case this is trouble and get a look."

We needed to find out what was happening. We couldn't return to the others and say we saw something but didn't know what it was.

I had a weird foreboding feeling in my gut. I didn't say anything about it to Nash, but I was certain he felt the same way.

The way he drove, through side streets to get to Beaver Road.

Beaver was a country road, four lanes, great shape, no potholes. Any businesses around there were spread out.

There were posted signs that the cargo entrance for the airport was ahead. We didn't see any other vehicles, but Nash was cautious. He parked in the AutoZone to scope the gated entrance across the road and when he saw it was clear, we drove there, parking just inside the gates.

I felt vulnerable, out in the open. We moved across the UPS hanger area like special ops, sticking close to the building, looking ahead.

On the third and final hanger, I peeked around, and saw we were close to the runway. We didn't need to get any closer, I felt we could see it all from there.

Before I could express that, Nash darted ahead, crouching down when he neared the bush lined area.

The bush area was a break area for employees, a few picnic tables that I didn't see from the flea market.

Signs saying to 'properly dispose of cigarette butts' were everywhere.

Nash was belly down looking through that bush and I was nearly under the picnic table to stay next to him,

I didn't need my binoculars to visually assess. There were so many planes, almost as if they brought them there. Twin engines, passenger planes, jets, some were old as well. If I was a bit more knowledgeable of history, I would have sworn there were World War Two planes there.

The soldiers did wear black. I didn't know if they were ours or not.

"I'm not seeing heavy artillery," Nash said. "That's a good sign."

"Yeah, but I'm not seeing any ambulances or anything medical."

"Or food, aid," Nash added.

"Right." I squinted as I peeked through my binoculars. "I can't make out who they are. There's a plane in the back that's not American. Can you see?"

"No." He grunted. "Hold on." After setting down the binoculars, awkwardly he twisted his body to pull the hunting rifle forward.

"What are you doing?"

"The scope on this is twenty times eighty. Way better than the binoculars. I should be able to see."

Like a soldier, he lay belly down, he peered down through the scope. "Okay that's better."

119

"Can you see?"

"I can."

"Who is it?" I asked.

"It's ... shit."

"What?"

Pop. Pop.

I heard it, the two gunshots and at first, I thought it was Nash who fired. But after a split second, the reality hit me that it came from the distance. Especially when I heard the rustle of the branch above my head. Instantly my body stiffened in fear as I looked to Nash. He shifted his eyes, they widened, and a singled stream of blood flowed down from his forehead a second before his head dropped.

I wanted to scream, that was my initial reaction. I felt it come out. But both my hands shot to my mouth to stifle it.

I was on my side, laying there next to him. Inches away. I heard voices shouting in the distance, I couldn't make out the words. I couldn't make out whether it was English or another language.

A quick look through the bushes and I saw four of them in the black military suits headed our way.

They had fired two shots. They saw both of us.

They move slowly, believing they got us both. No hurry. But I was.

I jolted quickly to back up, whacking my head on the picnic table. I literally saw stars and wasted a second or two getting it together. I then scooted hurriedly, away from that bush, staying low until I cleared enough when it was safe to stand.

I kept staring at Nash, just laying there, and I was leaving him. In my mind apologized. 'I'm sorry, I'm sorry this happened to you." I knew I would process it fully after I was out of there.

I was scared to death, and I didn't know why. Before it all, I wanted to die, now I just wanted to flee.

Once I knew it was safe to stand up, I did, and I ran. I ran fast until I got to the SUV. Once inside, keys still in the ignition, I didn't hesitate. I just took off.

TWENTY-FIVE
RUSHED

I was in such a hurry, I had driven at least three hundred feet before my door closed on its own.

I never closed it, I just fled.

Going back down Beaver Road scared me. What if they followed? I couldn't go back to the Motel Six, lead them to Stan. But if I didn't then Stan would come looking for us.

Oh, God, how do I tell them Nash was dead.

They shot us, they wanted us dead, which confirmed we were indeed in some sort of war.

Casting my eyes to the rearview mirror, I didn't see anyone follow me, but that didn't mean anything.

They had planes, all they had to do was fly overhead.

I made a hard right after the AutoZone, down a side street, then another right, driving insanely fast. Well, insanely fast for me.

My body was rigid as I clutched the wheel. My heart raced out of control and my breathing was heavy. A tense strain built up in my throat knocking into my jaw.

The vision of Nash played over and over in my head. His eyes moved, he was alive after that bullet went into him. He knew.

What did he see?

I looked in the rearview again then the side mirrors.

No one.

No vehicles.

I had to stop.

I just couldn't go any farther.

My foot slammed hard to the brake and I brought the vehicle to a screeching halt on a residential street.

The moment it stopped, I screamed.

Hard from my gut by way of my heart I screamed, and I just couldn't stop.

Screams filled with sadness, anger, fear. I cried out until my vocal cords waivered and grew hoarse.

I banged my hands, left, right, left right on the steering wheel, until I dropped my head to my hands on the wheel.

That's when I felt the moisture on the back of my hands.

I lifted my head and saw the blood.

With trembling fingers, I reached up and felt my head, I was bleeding from when I hit that picnic table.

The tears built, I felt that 'just about to cry' feeling until I shifted my eyes to the side view mirror and saw the approaching truck.

It was a good thing I hadn't put the SUV in park. I slid my foot from the brake, slamming it against the gas pedal and took off.

Now I was driving and looking. Forward then back, hoping I could lose them.

I made turns without thinking, not knowing where I was going. All I knew is that they were chasing me, and I couldn't lead them to the others.

Driving like a maniac was never really my forte. I didn't do it well and folded on the highway if I even got into the passing lane.

They were close, so close, but they weren't trying to get me. They were following, because without a doubt they could pass me. I just couldn't go fast enough.

A turn, then another, the tires screeched, and I realized I was just going in circles.

Finally, a turn and I knew that was it.

I saw the wreck ahead between a car and RV. It blocked the road, and my only recourse was to stop.

Unless I wanted to plow into them.

It wasn't the movies. I wasn't going to move them with the impact of the hit.

Hitting the brakes, I brought the SUV to a skidding stop, threw it in 'park', opened the door and jumped out.

They were going to shoot me. That's what I thought. I was out in the open, running for my life and they could pick me off like a sitting duck.

I needed to get behind the wreckage.

"Stop!" a male voice called out.

I slipped behind the RV to get around and was able to look back.

There were three of them.

A man and woman both in combat uniforms, they looked like American uniforms, the other man was wearing jeans and a tee shirt.

All were armed.

Once I made it passed the RV, I planned to just run.

Run and not do that bad horror movie thing and look back. I had to go, get close enough to warn Stan. Find a way to get them to hide.

They were in danger.

The man called out, "Stop!" again, but I didn't.

I looked at the houses that lined the road to my right. I aimed for them, planning on cutting through the yards, maybe getting to the next street and finding a place to hide.

Hearing him holler for me to stop put me in the mindset to expect a bullet to the back at any moment.

Just as I hit the grass, they got me. Not with a bullet, but bodily. One of them tackled me.

My shoulder slammed hard to the ground first, then my cheek. The weight of the person was on my back, and I squirmed to get free.

"Will you stop," the woman said. "Please. We aren't going to hurt you."

I didn't believe it, not at all. I still wiggled and fought.

"Stop," she repeated. "Now, I'm going to get up. Don't run. And don't scream. Noise travels and attracts."

"Then you shouldn't ..." I grunted and felt her body lift. I was freed and jumped up. "Shouldn't have shot my friend." I swatted at her when she reached for me.

"You're bleeding," she said.

I swatted again.

"And we didn't shoot your friend," she said.

The soldier man stepped forward. "We saw it happen. We were at the hangers watching as well. Trying to get intel on what they were doing. We didn't shoot at you. They saw you. They did."

The blue jean guy spoke up. "If we wanted you dead or to shoot you, we had plenty of chances, you don't run fast."

"Or drive fast," the woman added. "Let me look at your wounds, you have a lot of blood on your face. They shot twice, were you hit?"

"No." I shook my head. "I hit my head."

"We can't go back for your friend," the soldier man said. "They were on their way to him. How bad was he hurt?"

"He's dead."

"I'm sorry," he stated. "We need to get out of here now though. Before they start coming."

With a shuddering breath, spinning in confusion I stepped back. "They? You said they. They shot at us. Who is they?"

After looking at the woman and the other man, the soldier shook his head. "We don't know. We have no idea who they are. All we know," he said. "We've been invaded."

TWENTY-SIX
NEW FACES

I still didn't trust them, not one bit. The movie buff in me kept thinking they were lying to me that it was a trick to give our whereabouts. Like some spy movie.

They seemed nice enough, too nice. And it was awfully convenient that they just so happened to be nearby when Nash was shot.

Why weren't they shot at?

Poor Nash. He was so unsuspecting, and he didn't deserve what happened to him. The only positive of it was if there was a heaven or place where all good recently departed went, then Nash was with his family.

He grieved horribly for them. Put on a front for us, but I saw the pain he carried.

The three before me, like Stan didn't show much mourning in their actions.

Stan's was denial, maybe theirs was too.

I didn't bother getting their names or even giving mine. I had no plans to stick with them.

I knew them simply as Soldier man, Blue Jean Man and Kate. The only reason I knew her name was because they addressed her as Kate. She didn't say their names, maybe she didn't know them.

Both men were about the same age. Mid-twenties to early thirties. Soldier man looked military. Maybe it was just the uniform. He wasn't exceptionally tall, but he was big in presence. Blue Jean Man was an everyday looking guy. Kate was younger. Not much older than the drinking age.

No wonder she was so fast and spry. She wore a US Army uniform, but whether it was hers, I didn't know. Neither she nor the Soldier man wore the cover jacket that had the last name above a pocket.

There was something familiar about Blue Jean Man, I couldn't put my finger on it.

That still didn't matter, I needed to get away from them.

In the meantime, we sat inside the AutoZone, the vehicles parked a block away.

Kate cleaned the wound on my head and handed me a cold pack for my cheek.

My face wasn't the only thing that hurt.

My legs, my knees, my pride.

"Just wait for the planes," Kate said. "Once they make a pass, we're good for another two hours."

"Yeah," Blue Jean Man added. "They fly by every two hours and will make a second pass if they see someone. Probably reporting it."

"Damn," Soldier Man said with an exhale, then reached in his back pocket, pulling out a flask. "We are so far behind schedule." He took a drink and made an enjoyment gasp.

"Don't let me hold you up," I said. "I just need to get back to my group."

"How many are there of you?" Soldier Man asked.

I debated. Did I tell them there was four of us or did I lie and say we had a huge group? Just as I opened my mouth to speak, Soldier Man lifted his hand.

"Listen. Here they come."

The three of them all looked up to the ceiling as if it were glass and they could see the jets.

The closer they drew, the louder it was, and the more the floor vibrated.

"And there they go," Blue Jean Man said.

"Safe now," added Kate.

"Good." I stood. "Then this is where we part."

"What?" Kate said with a chuckle. "We all need to stick together. This is the only way we can get through the zone and fight."

Almost laughing, I replied. "Do I look like a fighter?"

"No, but you are."

"Let her go," Soldier Man said. "She doesn't trust us."

"I don't know you," I replied. "How do I really know you aren't the 'they' you keep talking about."

"I can prove I'm not," Kate said, then pulled from her back pocket what looked like a wallet. She flipped it open. "My military ID."

I glanced down to it, the picture matched her face and the name she gave.

Kate put it away. "I'm in the Army. We've seen hundreds of those soldiers from wherever over the last couple days. They wear black, some even look like freaking storm troopers. The US special forces when on an OP, yeah, they'll wear black, I don't think they're our guys. In general, it is not the widespread color of choice for combat uniform."

"Yeah," Blue Jean Man added. "Black is horrible for camouflage."

I met eyes with Kate. There was something in her eyes that made me suddenly start to trust her. Perhaps it was showing me her ID.

I agreed but on the condition we took both vehicles. We weren't that far from the Motel Six, it was pushing the time limit that Stan would come looking for me.

If he did decide to make the road trip, I wanted him to recognize the vehicle, not to mention, not feel threatened by a strange truck pulling up.

They agreed.

It took no more than seven minutes to return and just as I suspected, Stan was leaving to look for us.

The blue van was pulling out of the lot when I arrived and he stopped, stepping out immediately.

I did as well.

Then I saw it. The smile of relief dropped from Stan's face as he approached.

"Where's Nash?" Stan asked.

I shook my head.

"What does that mean?"

"He didn't make it. He was shot, Stan."

"Oh, dear Lord." He brought his hand to his mouth, then his eyes shifted from looking at me to behind me. "By them?"

"No. They found me when I was escaping. Long story, we'll all talk. They haven't told me much."

"Well, I'm sure… whoa." Stan paused. "Leave it to you to find Dan Matthews."

"Who?" I questioned, then it hit me. Dan from Bethe's. I spun around, sure enough Blue Jean Man was Dan. I knew he looked familiar. "Oh my God, that's him."

"You didn't know?"

I shook my head.

Kate, Dan and Soldier Man walked up to us.

"This is Stan. I'm guessing Renee and Nick are in the hotel," I said.

"That's right." Stan extended his hand. "You are Dan Matthews."

The corner of Dan's mouth raised some. "How...how did you know."

"We've been chasing you. Saw you in the video feed outside Bethe's. You left your license with your credit card."

"Yeah, I booked out of the city," Dan replied. "When I saw ... when I realized everyone was ... dead."

"I'll give your license and card back." Stan said. "I promise, I didn't use it."

"I believe that," Dan replied.

"Kate," she introduced herself with an extended hand. "Good to meet you Mister—"

"Miller, just call me Stan." He then turned to the Soldier Man. "You?"

"Sir, I'm Sergeant Bryce Owens," He replied. "You can call me Owens, Bryce, whatever you feel comfortable with. So, there are four of you?"

Stan nodded. "There were five."

"We're sorry for your loss," Owens said. "But glad you folks are alive."

"Thank you, Sergeant. Now, call it a gut instinct, but something tells me you three know more than us," Stan said. "Do you know what the hell is going on?

TWENTY-SEVEN
INTEL

"Kate and I were off base that Sunday evening," Owens explained his side of the events. "Having a beer, just got off duty when it started or rather when we received word that it had begun. It didn't happen all at once. It hit this area at approximately twenty minutes after ten. It started on the west coast thirty minutes earlier."

Kate continued the story. "It moved West to East along the jet streams. I mean right along the jet streams."

"We returned to base," Owens said. "We thought it was the safe thing to do and also knew we had about fifteen minutes before it hit us."

"This wasn't an act of nature," Kate said. "It was an attack, but from where it came from, we didn't know."

"The way people dropped dead," Owens added. "Told us it hit the brain or the heart."

"The brain," I said. "We did an autopsy."

"Really?" Owens said almost impressed. "That's good to know. Major Aberdeen was right, and he was just guessing. It was a pulse, like some unknown inaudible soundwave that beat its way across the US in less than an hour, coast to coast. There was no way to protect the heart if that's what it hit, but the Major was near certain if we protected the ears, it would possibly save lives."

Kate shook her head. "But it was upon us by the time he theorized that and no way to get the word out until he was near the East Coast. We don't know if we saved anyone, it was a Sunday night."

"I was wearing ear buds," Dan said. "That's how I survived, they told me."

Stan pointed to Kate. "You got yours on, I see."

Kate shook her head. "I didn't have any. That's also how we learned it was a low altitude, grounded thing. We were two hundred feet below the surface. Those in a basement level didn't survive."

It all confused me. "Why didn't we get breaking news? Surely if the west coast was hit, someone would have said something."

Renee chuckled. "Maybe they did. You wouldn't know. If I'm not mistaken, you had downed a bottle of pills with a vodka chaser and were dead to the world."

"That," Owen snapped a finger and pointed. "Is how you survived. The pulse worked opposite on anyone that had been dead less than five minutes. It was weird, it revived them. Like jump started the brain waves or heart."

"Ha," Stan blurted. "We're zombies."

"Pretty much," Owens said.

Nick finally spoke up. "You said low altitude? So, planes weren't affected?"

"Not the ones in flight," Owens replied.

"I thought that," Dan said. "Where were the plane crashes if everyone just dropped dead? I went to the airport."

"Our thoughts, too," Kate added. "We went out there and found Dan. Good thing. He told us about the invaders or soldiers in black."

"Loads of them," Dan stated. "There were passenger planes, but it was hard to tell if they had just landed or what happened to those onboard. I haven't heard a plane except the fighter jets. They landed somewhere."

"I agree." Then Stan questioned. "Is it just you three? Did anyone else on base live?"

Owens nodded. "Just those who were there, and we were on skeleton crew. So, there's fifteen of us."

"Soldiers in black?" Stan asked. "Like special ops. Almost every country uses black for special ops, even ours. And they all look the same, well, the Taiwanese cover their faces and the Delta Team in Peru look like those storm troopers from Star Trek."

"Star Wars," Dan corrected.

"Eh." Stan tossed out his hand. "Same difference."

The way everyone gasped at Stan's comment, you would have thought he committed an unforgivable offense.

"It doesn't make sense." Renee folded her arms close to her body, pacing and shaking her head. "We were attacked. We were invaded. Okay, they're winning. So why did they shoot Nash?"

Calmly, Stan replied, "We're at war."

"But why shoot a civilian?" Renee asked. "It doesn't make any sense."

"Nope," Owens replied. "You're right it doesn't. Civilians aren't generally shot, especially when they are unarmed."

I cleared my throat. "He ... he wasn't unarmed. I mean, Nash was armed. He was using the scope of a rifle to try to see the emblem on a plane."

Stan exhaled loudly. "Probably thought he was a sniper. Did he see the emblem?"

"He did but, he was shot before he could tell me what it was," I said. "Or rather who it was."

Stan looked at Owens. "Did you see the emblems?"

"We did." Owens looked at Kate, then answered, "For the last few days we have been surveying the airport. We saw a couple land and take off. Some are just sitting there."

"Okay," Stan said almost annoyed. "Well?"

"An older Russian fighter jet," Owens said. "Maybe from the eighties."

"Hot damn I was right," Stan snapped. "Didn't I tell you it was the crafty Russians."

"Plus," Owens said. "A jet from the royal air force, a beat-up F-14 and if I wasn't mistaken a World War Two Japanese fighter plane."

"Wait." Stan held up his hand. "What the hell did these people do? Hit the airplane museum out past Muncie? Because it sounds to me like that's what they did."

"Museum in Muncie?" I asked.

Stan nodded. "Yep, they have that airshow every year. Those planes work. It sure as heck sounds like it to me. They needed to work the air, they needed planes. And if that's the case, we may need to rethink the foreign invasion. Our attack may be a coup and came from within."

His words left us all stunned and thinking, at least they did for me.

Stan made a lot of sense, and he knew he captured the room with his theoretical wisdom. In the air of silence his microphone dropping moment left, Stan sought out his bottle.

TWENTY-EIGHT
ROLL OUT

We had moved from the Motel Six to the Super Walmart. It provided us with shelter and food. We hid the vehicles in the tire service garage.

The Walmart had lost power, like most places now. But it was the best place to hide out.

Plenty of camping gear, lanterns, and even a Coleman stove to cook our meal.

It was the first time I didn't feel like I was moving in circles. My thoughts were on the invasion and what role we could all play, instead of for once, how shitty of a person I was.

Then again, the snide comments and looks from Renee reminded me of that.

She was relentless and didn't stop. A bully waiting to be provoked.

She quieted down some since we joined the others.

For days, we hadn't seen anyone other than the new trio we traveled with.

As far as who they had seen, it was limited to the brigades of soldiers in black.

We had set up camp for the night, deep inside the store. Kate was on first watch and Nick joined her. Not that he could do much, but he wanted to feel like he was doing something.

I got that. I did, too.

Owens and Dan would switch out with them.

"There were areas not hit," Owens said, indicating to the map. "We know that. The pulse missed them, whatever. Several states down south."

"What about the people there?" Stan asked.

"Last we heard they set up perimeters, pulling all the soldiers, marines and civilians they could form a blockade. To protect what remains. Plan a counter strike."

"Are these soldiers in black doing anything to indicate they will invade the cities? I mean, we haven't seen any," Stan said.

"I know, it's just weird." Owens stated.

I glanced down to the map. Some areas were circled in green, I assumed those where the places not hit, a couple states and that surprised me. "Maybe they just wanted our heartland. You know to control farming." I shot a glance to Renee when she loudly scoffed at my comment.

Owens shook his head. "Then why wipe out Los Angeles and New York City."

"Well," Stan sung out the word. "I'll refrain from making a comment on that. But …. Have we heard anything from the enemy?"

"Nope," Owens replied. "Nothing. Then again, we may have. It's been two days since we communicated with Command."

"Why?" Stan asked.

"Until we knew we could have a secure line, it had to be radio silence."

Stan nodded. "Why did you stay behind?"

"Kate and I volunteered," Owens said. "Stay and get ground intel then head down. We've been checking airports."

Stan whistled. "There are a lot of airports in this area. Especially around Indianapolis. I mean, you checked more than Fort Wayne, right?"

"We did. Almost all. The little ones, the municipal ones, nothing. But the county ones, we saw smaller scale activity. Soldiers in black, trucks, small planes."

Renee asked. "Did you go into Indianapolis?"

Owens nodded. "We did. Well, the outskirts. It was hit."

"Here's what I don't get," I said. "Where are the passenger planes? The ones that didn't fall from the sky. Where are they? Did they land? Were they destroyed, if not where are the people?"

"I'm hoping," Owens said. "That when we get to command, they'll have answers. They've been in contact with NORAD. NORAD watches the sky; they'll know where those planes went. We'll get a lot more information when we get to Kentucky. I'm sure."

"Not enough." In frustration, Dan grunted and stood up. "Not enough information. We may get statistics but not answers. None of this makes a bit a sense to me. Nothing about it. Not to blow a hole in your coup theory, sir," he looked at Stan. "But if it was a coup, why aren't they making announcements? Blasting on the television or radio. Using a PA through the trucks. What do they want? In every movie and in real life, historically, there's an invasion, they sweep the streets. You have soldiers walking the streets. Fucking Hitler did that after the Blitzkrieg. What are they doing?

140

Not walking the streets. Gathering at airports with old planes and flying over."

I murmured. "Almost if they're waiting for something."

"Exactly." Dan pointed at me. "Like another hit."

"Another pulse?" I questioned.

"Now, now." Stan waved his hands. "Let's not get ahead of ourselves. I am sure there is more to this. And we can guess all we want, but we're in the dark until we get to Kentucky. Sergeant Owens, will we meet and talk to who is in charge down there?"

"Yes, we will, sir."

"Good. Good. Might I suggest," Stan said. "Instead of tossing out guesses, we write down questions that we have. It'll pass the time tonight. Keep your mind busy. Write them down. There's plenty of office supplies in aisle seven. Tomorrow, no matter how little the information, it'll be more than we have right now."

Oh, Stan.

He was a new acquaintance to me, but I adored him instantly. Maybe because he didn't know me, and he didn't judge. He was a plethora of wisdom and calm. I wanted to know more about him, and I would. Just like one day I would tell him about me and what I had done.

At that moment, our circle lit by dim lanterns, I thought of the questions I would write down. Questions I hoped would get answered the next day.

It wasn't that long to wait.

We would leave at first light.

TWENTY-NINE
FOUND

For the sake of fuel and the fact we didn't have many supplies, the seven of us loaded into one SUV. What we had between the truck and SUV in gas would get us to Fort Knox.

I volunteered to sit in what Stan called the 'rumble seat', the third row. He sat back there with me, and it was quite the challenge getting in and out. It wasn't like a minivan. We had to open the hatch, folded the one seat while Stan climbed in. I did the same then unfolded seat seven and sat down.

It wasn't that far. Two hundred miles. Hopefully, I wouldn't have to get back out until we arrived.

Stan didn't have to sit back there, Dan offered, as did Kate, but Stan wanted to.

It sat two people. The seat was hard, and it had very little leg room. Our knees touched the row in front and our view was limited to the tiny windows on our side.

It did have one benefit.

I couldn't hear a word anyone said.

Like sitting in the back of the plane, the only person I heard was Stan.

He announced that, too.

"No one try to talk to us; we can't hear you!"

He wanted me to look at the notes he took, questions he had for when we arrived at Fort Knox, but I was one of those people who couldn't read while in a car because I'd get sick.

Instead, Stan verbally told me about each item.

A few of them would trigger memories of Bess his wife, but she was the only family member he spoke about. I knew he had a slew of kids and grandchildren.

I never pushed him to talk about them, especially since he was placing himself in the mindset that they were still alive, and he walked out on them.

"Look at this. He worked at that Walmart." Stan showed me an ID. "You know he's from Kentucky. Never changed his license. Maybe he was in school, and his parents are at this address. Not all of Kentucky was hit. Maybe I can find them."

"I'll go with you."

"Thank you. They will want his stuff. I got it out of his locker. He had some marijuana, they may need it."

I sadly chuckled.

"Jonah Lawrence. Nineteen." Stan shook his head. "Nineteen is too young to die."

Instantly my thoughts went to Stephanie who was also nineteen. "You're right. Nineteen is far too young." After drifting in thoughts for a second, I snapped out. "Stan what did you do for a living. I assume you retired."

"Somewhat. I volunteered a lot. I was a lawyer."

"And you volunteered?" I asked.

"After I left my practice. Yep. For the Innocence Project."

"You are a defense attorney?"

"One of the best defense lawyers in the state." He glanced at me. For a second, a split second, I thought he knew.

Maybe I was wrong.

"I helped a lot of people," Stan said.

"Did you ever …"

I stopped talking and he and I looked up when the SUV slowed down and pulled over.

"What's going on?" I asked loudly.

Nick replied. "I have to take a leak."

Nick opened the rear door and climbed out.

"Where the hell is he going?" Stan asked, looking out his window.

Nick walked off the side of the road and from sight. "Maybe he wants privacy."

"Oh, just turn your back. No one cares. Anyhow …" Stan said. "You were asking me something?"

"Yes. Did you ever help someone that actually committed the crime?" I asked.

"Depends on what you mean by help? I helped those who admitted their guilt, but not to get free. To get help. I had a mother forty years ago that took the lives of her three young children, all under six. Drown them. It was post-partum psychosis. Everyone in her family disowned her. Everyone. Her husband left her. We weren't trying to get her free, just help. She didn't want to be free. She had to live with that and no one forgiving her."

His words caused a lump in my stomach, and I pursed my lips. "Stan, I—"

"What the hell is taking him so long?" He leaned forward. "Owens go check on him. It's taking too long to take a whiz."

"Yes, sir."

The second Owens stepped out, so did Kate, then Renee and Dan.

"They're leaving us?" Stan asked.

"I'm getting us out of here. If we have to bolt, we can't do it from the back seat."

I climbed over to the second row and stepped out. When I did, I could hear them calling for Nick. Something was wrong, I felt it.

I opened the back hatch and folded the seat for Stan to climb over. When he did, I helped him out.

"Is he lost?" Stan asked.

"I don't know."

"Guys!" Nick called from the distance. "You have to see this."

We walked over to the portion of the road where the others stood, where Nick had climbed over the guardrail and vanished to relieve himself.

As we joined the others, Nick emerged from the bush lined area. "You have to see this. You have to."

Everyone climbed over that guardrail. I helped Stan to make sure he didn't fall, and we followed Nick who moved quickly.

I thought perhaps he was running through the woods, but the side of the road bushes wasn't thick, and it was fifty feet until the steep hill.

It gave a view of what was below. A four-lane secondary road that I was certain crossed the highway we took at some point. Open fields and farmland, waiting for planting, graced both sides.

But the farms, the fields and the roads weren't what Nick called us for.

It was the dozen passenger planes all parked there.

Different airlines, different sizes, but all passenger planes. They weren't in any order, but they all had their landing gear down.

It was obvious they didn't crash, they landed and taxied there.

They had to be some of the missing planes that were in flight when the pulse hit.

But why there? Why were they just left there? And more importantly, what happened to the passengers?

THIRTY
HOLLOW AND FULL

We had to get down there. No, we all *wanted* to get down there. That large hillside gave a vast view, none of the soldiers in black were anywhere around. But it also was deceiving. It was a lot farther away than it looked.

Owens pulled out the map. To get to the planes, we needed to turn around, head back north, four miles then after the exit take a series of side roads to get there.

There was also the option of going down the hill and walking there, but Stan couldn't make that, and he certainly couldn't make it back up.

I volunteered to take the SUV with Stan and meet those who wanted to walk.

It was just him and I that took the vehicle.

It was the first time in a long time that Stan and I were alone. I really debated at that moment to tell him the truth. Tell him about me, what I had done and why I wanted to die.

After hearing he was a defense lawyer, I believed he wouldn't judge me. But a part of me didn't want to disappoint Stan, to let him down or lose his faith.

I was a coward, I had my moment in the back of the SUV waiting on Nick and I couldn't tell him.

The moment was gone.

The highway was mostly barren, a few cars here and there. Sunday night traffic on a non holiday weekend.

It was easy. Not that we could pick up speed and cruise on by. I never knew when something was blocking the road.

We didn't bother going to the other side of the highway. Why would we? We were the only ones on the road.

It wouldn't be that way in forty miles when we arrived in Kentucky.

The dead empty earth we had been living in for nearly a week would be behind us.

We took the exit and found the turns that eventually took us to the road where we would find the plane. It was a bit more than four miles. Not much.

"Did you know," Stan said. "At any given time, there are thousands of planes in the air."

"I didn't know how many," I replied.

"Yeah, you were right when you said it. Where did they all go. I mean this is only twelve."

"Maybe they radioed each other and met up."

"There's something bigger, Vivian, there really is."

"What do you mean?" I asked.

"I mean, take a look at everything that happened and is happening. It has to be more than ..." Stan stopped. "Whoa. Stop."

"What? Why?" We were still at least two miles from those planes.

"Look."

I didn't see them at first, but once Stan drew my attention, I did and drove the SUV closer.

About a hundred feet ahead in what could have been mistaken for a hillside was a mound of luggage.

A huge mound of luggage.

I didn't pull off the road, but I pulled to the side and we both stepped out.

It was as if someone had not only taken every piece of luggage and tossed them in a mountainous pile, but they were picked through. Bits of clothes were scattered about, and it appeared that every suitcase had been opened.

I didn't want to sound like an idiot by stating the luggage had to come from the dozen planes, that went without saying.

"If we're seeing this," Stan said. "I wonder what we will find out on that plane."

We got back in the SUV and continued down the road.

The planes had landed.

Unless it was some sort of passenger plane graveyard that we were reading too much into, then those planes in the field, parked randomly, had all landed.

If they landed the pilot was alive.

The passengers had to be alive.

We didn't see any signs of people at all.

Not long after leaving the luggage find, we made it to the planes.

We pulled up and Owens was standing in the open door of a 737. In fact, all the doors were open, but there were no staircases, no emergency ramps deployed.

If the people left the planes, how did they get out?

How did Owens get up there?

It was after I stopped that I saw he had crawled in the cargo door.

He shook his head sadly to us, then a few moments later, he came out.

"All dead," he announced.

"Everyone?" I asked.

"Everyone. Even the pilot."

"How did a dead pilot land a plane?" Stan asked. "Bet me there was no luggage in the cargo."

"How did you know?" Owens questioned.

Stan pivoted back with a point. "It's all back there. The enemy went through it."

Kate spoke up. "We need to check the other planes, just to be sure. All the cargo gates are open. We need to check the planes."

She was right. As much as I didn't want to, I was curious.

We would split up.

I went with Dan. Kate with Renee and Owens and Nick paired off.

There were eleven more to check.

Stan opted to stay back and be look out. He wanted to go but after realizing he had to crawl up a small space with a ladder, he declined.

I was nervous and knew when Dan and I entered the large plane that once we emerged to the main cabin it wasn't going to smell pretty. I braced myself for that.

"Was there really all that luggage?" Dan asked as we walked through the empty cargo bay. It was dark, lit only by the sun that peeked through.

"Yeah, there was. It was picked through."

"What the hell?"

"I know. Maybe Fort Knox will have the answers."

"Maybe. I'm not holding my breath that all is well there."

"Why?"

"The world fell apart days ago. You think those who survived are handling it all that well." He stopped at a ladder. "I'll go up and do the hatch."

"Okay." I nodded.

Dan climbed the ladder. I could hear him grunt as he struggled with something. Then I heard the floor door open.

I stayed at the bottom looking up.

"Oh, God. Brace yourself. It's bad up here." He coughed.

I lifted my tee shirt over my nose, not that it would do anything, and I climbed up.

Even though I tried my best, the horrendous smell of death hit me as soon as I neared the top.

It was no wonder. A dead male flight attendant was right there. He sat on the floor, his back against the cabinet in the galley and his feet mere inches from the hatch,

Dan extended his hand to me to help me the rest of the way.

"A quick look," he said. "See if we can determine how they died, see if anyone is alive and then we're out."

I nodded, holding my shirt against my nose.

He moved ahead. We were in the back. Dan pushed open the lavatory doors to check, then before I followed, I glanced back at the flight attendant.

That look. The look on his face. That surprised painful look that was on everybody I had seen that dropped dead instantly.

But he was in a further state of decay. His body greenish and bloated.

It wasn't bright in the plane, but light enough to see. The window shades were all up.

A single narrow aisle went through the plane with three seats on both sides.

Dan walked slowly a few rows ahead of me, looking left to right.

Not every seat was full. There were a lot of empty seats. It was about ten rows into my walk I noticed no one was wearing seatbelts. They all were in their seats, most of their heads back against the rest, some had slumped forward.

Had they all died by the pulse? It looked it and if so, how did the pilot land the plane.

Toward the middle, my foot kicked something, and I looked down.

It was a doll.

Dodi Dinosaur. A popular children's cartoon about a little dinosaur girl.

It just laid there. I closed my eyes for a moment and groaned painfully.

The children.

My God, the children that had died.

Knowing it was right there at aisle thirteen, I couldn't look. I didn't want to see.

Dan stopped at the front and turned around. "Where are the women?"

"What?" I looked at him.

"There are no women. Every single body is a man."

Hurriedly I spun around. I hadn't even noticed. He was right. Glancing back down to that doll, I immediately looked left and right and to the back.

"Or children," I said. "There are no children. But ..." I bent down and lifted Dodi. "There's this."

"What the hell?" Dan said. "I mean this wasn't a flight of all men. The empty seats. They had to be the women. Where are they? This plane landed. These men were killed after. They aren't all buckled in. Why would they do this?"

Dan was full of questions, the same ones I had. We'd have to see if the other planes were similar.

"Unfortunately," I replied. "We will never know what …" As those words slipped from my mouth, I glanced down and saw it.

Passenger in the middle seat of row thirteen.

A young man, his head slumped to the side and in his hand was a phone.

The screen was black, it was dead, but he held it as if he had been using it and his hand just dropped.

We had lived in a day and age when nothing went unnoticed, when no disturbance went unrecorded.

Had he recorded something?

I reached down for it, prying his rigid fingers.

It could have been nothing, but it could also be answers to what happened on that plane.

It was worth a shot, and we'd find out when and if we powered up that phone.

THIRTY-ONE
HARD KNOCKS

Inspired by Stan or wanting to make him proud, whatever it was, I checked the pockets of the young male passenger in aisle thirteen for some sort of identification.

Nothing.

I would have to wait until I undid his phone and then maybe Stan could add him in the notebook as another person whose life was snuffed and, in some way, helped us.

I was sure and convinced that the phone he held had the answers. That he was recording up until he died.

There had to be answers. There had to be time to record because every plane was the same.

No female bodies.

No bodies of children.

Those planes were coaxed to land in one area, to gather and park, I was sure of it. The area was too odd for them to coincidentally be there.

The enemy, the soldiers in black brought them there.

Then they took the women and children and killed the men.

Which was scary because it looked as if they all died by the pulse. Which meant, they had a means to deliver it on a smaller scale.

The only positive was that the women and children were missing. They were taken. They had to be alive somewhere.

The planes were a revelation and a find none of us wanted to be a part of, yet we were, and we carried this information with us as we drove to Kentucky.

I wasn't sure what I was thinking when Owens said some states were spared. As if those who released the pulse were like, 'we can skip this state and that state'.

States that were spared didn't mean the entire state, but a large portion of it was missed.

We just didn't see any people, signs of life at all.

There was supposed to be people in Fort Knox and the town of Louisville wasn't touched.

Owens had confirmed that with his team that went down.

But as we approached Louisville, we had to take an alternate route.

Thick black smoke rose to the sky, indictive of fires and destruction, signs of war.

Though we saw no war planes, or signs of the soldiers in black, to me, it had to be their ground movement.

Louisville had not been spared by the invasion.

Again, that's what I had thought.

It wasn't the case.

As much as it sounded like a cliché, getting into Fort Knox was tough. The four-person guard team put us through the ringer, and finally they let us in to be taken to Major Aberdeen.

For some reason when I heard the name Major Aberdeen, I expected some older guy, maybe way overdue for a promotion and angry about it.

Instead, Aberdeen was a nice-looking man, younger as well. Not sure why I thought Army officers were old.

The major seemed really happy to see Owens and Kate, greeting them with a warm embrace after the obligatory salute.

"I am so happy you made it," Aberdeen said. "I was worried."

"We would have been earlier today," said Owens. "But we had to get around Louisville. Was it attacked?'

"Nope," the major replied. "Riots."

"Riots?" Owens asked.

"Yep. All over the city. They took down our perimeter as if we were the enemy. They're angry and they don't know much so they are rioting. We pulled out. I wasn't risking any of my soldiers."

I asked, "When did it start? The rioting I mean?"

"Two days ago."

I looked over to Dan when I remembered what he said on the plane.

"We'll head to the command room," Aberdeen said. "I want to debrief you folks. All of you if you don't mind."

Stan spoke up. "We have questions too."

"If I can answer them, I will. Nothing that's classified, just we don't have much. But I am glad Owens found you folks."

"We found a lot of things," Owens said. "Like a dozen planes just sitting there. They landed and I don't know if they kind of taxied in that position or what."

Aberdeen didn't say anything about that, he nodded then led us down a hall to a meeting room and stood in the door while we all walked in.

He closed the door. "Have a seat. Please." He held out his hand. "You said a dozen planes?"

"Yes," Owens replied. "Strangest thing. All the bodies were men. No women or children."

"There are other planes, too. NORAD said, only eight percent of the planes in the air dropped from the sky. So, a small percentage crashed. The rest landed."

"Did they know where?" Owens asked.

"Yes, but at this point manpower is limited. To be honest, you have given the first report."

"I found this." I lifted the phone I retrieved off the plane. "It was in one of the passenger's hands. It's dead, but he may have been texting or recording."

"Thank you." Aberdeen took it. "That's really good thinking. We'll find a way to charge it and check."

Dan interjected. "They looked like they were hit with the same thing that killed most of the people."

Aberdeen huffed a slow breath. "Almost like they have a portable version of their weapon?" He shook his head. "We don't have the technology. Someone does. It's just so far advanced."

"Damn Russians," Stan commented.

Renee who had been silent spoke sheepishly. "Please don't laugh. Could it be an extraterrestrial life form that did this?"

"I'm not laughing," said Aberdeen. "But unless they have Type-O blood and are replicas of us, it's not aliens."

"Wait," Owens said. "Type-O blood."

Aberdeen nodded. "We captured one. Hoping to get information."

Stan laughed. "You aren't getting info from a grunt. He's probably bottom of the barrel. Reminds me of that old movie Independence Day where they interrogate a grunt alien, and he just spews forth the mission statement."

"I'm not sure we even have gotten that," Aberdeen said.

"Is he not talking?" asked Owens.

"Oh, he's talking. But manpower again is short, and we don't have an interpreter. We haven't a clue what he's saying."

"What language?" Owens asked.

"Bet me it's Russian," Stan said.

"Um." Aberdeen looked at Stan. "We believe it's Russian."

"Ha!" Stan chimed.

I lifted my hand. "I speak Russian."

Stan spun to me. "You speak Russian?"

I nodded. "My mother insisted we learn a language, I learned Russian. I can try to speak to him if you want. If he's speaking Russian, I'll understand him."

The Major's face lit up and he smiled. "Absolutely. Yes. Let's take you to him now."

Stan gave me a swat on the arm with a 'good girl' comment and while the others stayed behind, I left with the Major.

It felt good to be able to help. And I was curious as to what he had to say ... if anything.

THIRTY-TWO
DEVON

I had never been in the military, and I never had any desire until the second I realized we had been attacked.

From that moment on I just wanted to be a part of whatever it took to fight back.

Aberdeen talked every step of the way. Not a moment was silent from the second we left the meeting room until we arrived two buildings over where the holding area was located.

"He was one of three," Aberdeen stated. "The other two were fatally wounded and didn't make it. We tried. We tried to save them. You can't get information out of a dead man."

"I understand."

"There are two ways to go about things," Aberdeen said. "You can take the hardcore approach, or you can try to gain his trust."

"Good cop, bad cop."

"Yes. Sometimes trust can go a long way. I don't expect you to know much about getting information from prisoners."

"I was able to get information from children," I said.

"What do you mean?"

"I was a pediatric nurse and sometimes I had to talk to kids to get the truth."

"Talking to the young will come in handy."

"What do you mean?"

"He's young."

I nodded. "Major, I know there's no recruitment center, but I want to be a part of the fight. I want to help."

"This is part of the fight."

"In any way I can help, know that I am here."

We arrived at the interrogation room, there was a guard on the door and before heading in, I looked through the two-way mirror into the room.

He sat in his black uniform, hands cuffed staring out, looking so lost and I saw how young he was.

Having been a pediatric nurse, I was good at guessing ages and the young man in there was no older than fifteen.

"Oh my God," I whispered and looked at the major. "He's a child."

"I know."

"A child-soldier."

"That he is, and he was armed."

"He is scared. He is really scared," I said. "Have you … Have you thought about using the uniforms to infiltrate?"

"We have but, again, a communication problem is at hand."

"Perhaps we can break that." I glanced at the soldier. "Look at his face. Maybe good cop bad cop isn't the answer."

"What do you mean?"

"I know kids. Even though I'm not a mom, maybe just be the good cop," I said. "Let me go in there and gain his trust. Let me talk to him. Can you hear me out here?"

"Yeah, but it won't make a hill of beans if you're speaking Russian."

"Can you record this?" I asked.

"I can."

"Record it and I'll translate it all. If I go in there and just talk without telling you what is said, he may trust me enough to tell me something."

"It's worth a shot."

"Before I go in there, can you get me two cans of soda? One for me and one for him?"

Aberdeen sighed out annoyed and agreed. I wanted an olive branch, and he was a teenage boy, absolutely a can of Pepsi would do the trick.

He gazed at the can when I extended it as if he had never seen it before. Maybe he was one of those child soldiers raised to only be a soldier.

It was my nonverbal greeting which he didn't take.

"Voz'mi eto. Eto napitok," I told him to take the can that it was a drink.

He stared up at me.

I asked in Russian if he spoke Russian, but then he shook his head no.

"Vy ponimayete menya?" I asked if he understood me.

He nodded.

"We're off and running."

161

I pulled out a chair and sat, showing him my soda then opening the can. The 'snap' of it caused him to jerk some and he watched as I sipped mine. I then reached over and open his.

I nodded. "Go on."

Apprehensively he took a small sip. I could tell by his reaction he really didn't know what to make of the bubbly and sweet beverage. He sipped it a few more times.

"Vivian." I placed my hand to my chest. "My name is Vivian." I pointed at him.

With almost a scared and shaky voice, he replied. "Devon."

Wanting to know where he was from, I asked, "Otkuda ty?"

He had said he wasn't from Russia so perhaps he was from Kazakhstan or Ukraine any of the number of places where Russian is the main language.

"Net strany. Net strany. My vse kak odin," he replied.

His reply was odd. No Country? They were as one? I started to speak again, then his young age blasted through as he grew emotional.

"YA khochu nayti svoyego ottsa. YA khochu svoyego ottsa."

He was asking for his father. So, I questioned if his father was a soldier, or was he home.

Devon nodded, not really answering the question. It wasn't yes or no.

His emotions and fear intensified, and he said in his language, "I don't want to die. I don't want to die. I want my father."

162

Using my best calm voice, I lifted my hand and spoke gently to him as best as he could understand. "We'll find your father. You're not going to die. We aren't going to hurt you."

At that moment his reaction surprised me. Maybe it was the sugar from the soda. In an angry saddened response, he jumped up, slamming his hands and knocking over his soda as he yelled out. "Ty uzhe mertv. Vse mertvy. My pytayemsya spasti gryadushchikh."

It didn't make any sense what he was saying, it didn't fit into the narrative., Lips pursed trying to think of my question, the door opened.

Aberdeen's presence brought silence. "Can I see you?"

"Yeah." I glanced at Devon. "Yeah." I stepped to the door and paused when Devon started to yell again.

"My pytayemsya spasti mir," he shouted passionately.

I slipped into the hall, closing the door, my mind was still on what Devon had just said.

"Major, I know it's only been a few minutes," I explained. "But he was saying..."

"I didn't pull you out for lack of trying. I want you to come with me."

"What's going on?" I asked.

"That phone you grabbed. It powered up. You were right," the major said. "He recorded it all."

THIRTY-THREE
ON THE WALL

For a moment I thought I was pretty important, being snapped from interrogation because something I thought to do panned out.

I still don't know why I thought about that phone. Maybe it was the countless videos always online about things happening on planes.

We left the building where they held Devon and returned to the main command, where I was led into an even bigger meeting room.

This one had a television screen on the wall.

I was alone in that room for about ten minutes when Stan, Renee, Nick and Dan were escorted in.

"You okay, kid?" Stan asked.

"I am, thanks. The phone worked out," I said.

"That's what I heard. That's why we're here, right?" Stan asked.

Before I could answer, Dan did. "Bet they can't understand what is being said. Otherwise, this would have been a secret."

"Do we want to know what they said?" Renee asked. "I mean, does it matter."

"Yes." Stan nodded. "It does. Viv, did you talk to the soldier?"

"I did. He's a boy, Stan. Maybe fifteen. Scared to death. Calling for his father."

"Huh." Stan stepped back. "Odd."

"Why is that?" I questioned.

"When under duress or in trouble," Stan said. "Most men, boys, call out for their mothers."

Nick suggested. "Maybe he doesn't have a mother. Maybe the taking of women has something to do with it."

Stan pointed at Nick. "That's a good point. Viv, what did he say?"

I was ready to tell him when the door opened and Aberdeen, Owens and Kate stepped in.

"You hit the jackpot," Owens said. "Of course, you know, there are parts we need you to translate."

"What did I tell you?" Dan asked. "We want to see it all. Not just the translate parts."

"Absolutely." Owens set down the phone, which was connected to a portable charger. He then searched out a remote and turned on the television.

"Did you get a name?" Stan asked. "Anything on that phone. I keep track."

Kate nodded. "Yes, his name was Ben Durella. From Atlanta, but that was all he had in the about me section of his phone."

Aberdeen stepped forward. "Everyone have a seat. Ben started recording after they landed. Owens can you cast that to the TV?"

Owens reached for the phone. "Yes, sir."

I sat next to Stan who leaned forward giving all his attention to the screen.

"Can you turn that up, please?" Stan requested.

From the camera's lens, it was just passengers seated.

"So here we are, we finally landed," Ben narrated. "Nearly, out of fuel. They aren't really saying much. People have tried to call home. Only one woman managed to make a connection. Something happened. Like an attack. But according to the pilot we were told to land here."

Owens paused the video. "He has like more without any real information, just what they served to eat. About people trying to find information. This one is interesting."

The next video started with a view out of the window. "Not sure if this is seen," Ben said. "But look at all those planes. Two were here when we arrived, the others just showed up. The Captain said they were told the same thing. To land on this highway. We taxied off to the side to leave it open for other planes. I'm trying to save battery. I'll record more when I find anything out."

It jumped to the next video which started as a shaking camera in the middle of commotion. Voices shouting, women yelling, a child could be heard crying. Some of the voices sounded as if they were begging and pleading. And mixed in with it, I recognized the Russian language. There were several of the soldiers in black. But I couldn't see them too clearly. Just parts of their uniforms.

"They did get on the plane," Aberdeen said. "What are they saying?" he asked me.

"They're preaching calm," I replied. "That one man keeps saying it's a rescue and they're getting the women and children first."

Like Stan, I leaned forward with intent at the screen. The soldiers walked down the aisle, pointing then extending hands to women to exit the row.

"Okay," Ben said. "They're taking the women and children. They're being gentle, not raising weapons. I think something is happening and they are evacuating them first. I don't understand. It sounds like Russian." Ben's voice slowed down when the one soldier, the man that had done most of the talking, walked down the aisle. It was then I noticed they wore helmets and shielded their faces.

The man looked at the camera, even though Ben lowered it some, and kept on walking.

I glanced at Aberdeen. "Were the three that were captured wearing helmets, too?"

"Yes, they were."

Ben spoke on the video. "I guess they don't care that I'm recording. I'll keep it going. I'm on eight percent. I hope this stays on."

It didn't take long, all the women were removed orderly and calmly. Then every soldier but the main guy left.

He stood at the front for a moment, then looked to the door as two soldiers returned and stood there. He spoke loudly.

"Spasibo za zhertvu."

I murmured, "He thanked them for their sacrifice."

"My God," Stan said. "They do kill them. This confirms they have a smaller version of this weapon."

"Where?" Dan asked. "I don't see it."

"Maybe the two in the door have it," Owens said. "We left and came back."

The main soldier headed toward the door.

Another male voice called out, "I don't like this. Are we gonna die? Are you killing us?"

He stopped as if he understood. I know he did, because he replied, repeating almost verbatim what Devon had said, "Vy vse uzhe mertvy. My spasayem mir."

The video went black.

The room felt silent.

Major Aberdeen took the floor and stood at the end of the table. "There is something far deeper going on. I think all of you know this. Vivian, what was he saying at the end?"

"He said almost exactly when Devon said," I replied. "Devon repeated it. We are dead already and they are saving the world."

Everyone erupted with audible confusion noises.

"What the hell does that mean?" Stan asked.

"It seemed out of place when Devon said it," I answered. "I told him we weren't hurting him. But that ..." I pointed to the screen. "That man knew English. A guy from the plane asked if they were killing them and he said they were dead already."

I watched Stan slump back.

"Vivian," the major said. "You told me you wanted to be part of this fight."

"I do."

"You brought up infiltration using their uniforms."

I nodded. "It would be easier now with the masks."

Renee grunted. "Oh my God, why are you acting like she is some military guru?"

Stan wagged his finger at her. "You need to be nice."

"She's not a military guru," the major said. "She does know the language."

168

Before any more was said, Stan grunted out a, "no."

"Vivian," the major said. "You know the language and can wear Devon's uniform. Would you be willing to go with Sergeant Owens to sneak in and find out what is going on?"

"Say no," Stan told me.

I couldn't. Of the massive wrong I had done in my life, I could finally do some good.

"Vivian," Stan spoke with concern. "This can get you killed."

I reached over and placed my hand on Stan's. "And I'm okay with that. So ..." I glanced up to Aberdeen. "I'll do it."

THIRTY-FOUR
TAKING INSURANCE

Owens was frustrated. He didn't come across as a man that let little things get to him, but Devon's inability to show us on the map, just rubbed him the wrong way.

"Tell him he and his people came here. He has to know where they are located, at least one, he's a soldier."

"All that. You want me to say all that."

"Where?" Owens spoke slow and strong, his finger hitting the map with every syllable. "Where are your people?

"That's not gonna do it. He's scared and sad."

"I don't care."

I faced Devon. "Where are your people? Gde tvoi lyudi?"

"My vash narod."

"What did he say?" Owens asked.

"We *are* your people."

"What the hell?"

"Bozhiy narod."

I translated for Owens. "God's people."

"Oh, come on," he groaned. "Really. I didn't think Russians believed in God."

That made me laugh. "What?"

"Yeah, aren't they like an atheist country?"

"No!" I clapped back in disbelief. "Ever hear of Russian Orthodox?"

"Ok, for some reason ... never mind." He shook his head. "We need direction, Viv. We need..."

"YA khochu poyti k svoyemu ottsu," Devon cut him off.

"What did he say now?"

I sighed out. "He wants to go to his father."

"Yeah, well, you can have ... Dad ... when you tell us where to find him. I'll bring you his body."

"Oh, my God, stop," I told him. "Like him, his father is a grunt in this... whatever you want to call it. But ... but you gave me an idea."

"No."

"What? I didn't even say what it was."

"I know what you're gonna say. It's not gonna work."

"No, you don't," I argued.

"I do."

"Then tell me," I said. "Tell me what my idea is."

"You wanna tell him if he wants to go to his dad, he has to tell us where he is."

"No," I barked. "That's not what I'm gonna say. I was gonna say if he tells us where his father is, we'll take him."

"The major will never approve."

"The major is in charge here, but the people on the mountain are calling the shots. And they'll agree to anything that gets us there." I glanced at Devon then back to Owens. "Give me five minutes."

171

I tried to hide my smug expression when I went to the office to meet with the major and Owens. I probably didn't do a good job. I placed the map down on the table. "Hiding in plain sight. Outskirts of Nashville. That's where one is. That's where his father is. They have a base there."

"Nashville?" the major asked. "That was hit by the pulse. Did he say how many cities they were in. Bases?"

I shook my head. "No, he wouldn't give any more information than his base. There's about two hundred soldiers there so we can blend in really well. It's only a two-hour drive, but we will need to walk to the base since he said the foot soldiers don't have vehicles."

Owens stood with arms crossed. "So, we get close enough and walk in. How do we know he's being honest with you?"

"Because we're taking him."

Owens laughed, then turned serious. "No, we aren't. You said you were just telling him that."

"Yes. He believes me. If he didn't and was lying, he'll change his tune the second we take him."

"It could be a trap," Owens said.

"He is not high enough up the ladder to coordinate an attack. He wants his father," I said. "Let's take him."

The major exhaled with a shake of his head. "The second you walk onto their base with him, he'll give you away. Guaranteed."

"I thought of that," I said. "Owens and I walk onto base in uniform. We get close enough to walk there and leave Devon behind with maybe Dan and Kate to watch him. He will be our assurance if Owens and I get busted."

The major asked, "Did he give you a location?"

"He did not, but I think I know where they are. He said it was a large, abandoned building that had many empty rooms that were shops."

The major's expression changed from doubt to a look of revelation. "A mall. Nashville, it has to be the one on Hickory Hollow Road. They could have even arrived and hid there before the pulse."

"Or," Owens said, "maybe the weapon is there."

"Hopefully," the major circled the area with his finger. "You two can find out."

I was proud of what information I was able to obtain and how my mind was able to snap into some sort of mode. It probably was from watching all those old war movies with my mother and father. Whatever the reason, I was glad to contribute and even more happy that I would be a physical part of it.

THIRTY-FIVE
FREE

It was a lot more in depth than I thought it would be. We were to find out if they had the weapon, if they planned on using it again and hopefully, the end game.

Blend in.

Dress as the soldiers, say very little and follow a pack.

Owens and I were both given tracking devices that locked into the missiles controlled at Cheyenne mountain.

Once we had the information we needed and were clear of the base, they were going to destroy it.

The first counterattack.

We would drive to a location outside of Nashville and camp for the night, leaving Dan and Kate with Devon when we walked at first light.

Owens and I would wear the uniforms just in case we came across any soldiers in black. We could claim they were prisoners.

The uniform felt weird. It was a thick, coarse material. I wore Devon's. While I was never really healthily endowed in the breast department, I taped them down just to be safe.

In those moments of getting dressed, being alone with the mission on my mind, I thought of a lot of things.

I knew without a doubt, there was a good chance I would die.

It was hard to reconcile my life, because so much was left that I could never reconcile or put behind me.

If I died, I would die a broken woman that broke so many people. They, like me, died before they could get relief, find peace.

Unlike when I tried to take my life, my mind was clear enough to think of everything.

I thought of my mother and realized that I never really gave her any credit. She tried after my father died to be the best she could, she never remarried, and I hoped she wasn't lonely when she died. At least she didn't have to live to go through my brother's death.

Because of my mother's tough rules, I was able to help out my country, and that would have made her proud.

I missed Louis. Then again, I missed my husband before he died. I had come to terms that he wasn't happy, that he found someone else. I couldn't come to terms with losing my best friend since we were in the seventh grade.

He knew he had hurt me and tried to be my friend, but it wasn't the same. I didn't have that shoulder to lean on at my beck and call. Renee had him and I just had a hard time fathoming why she hated me so much.

That she put on such a façade, I believed she was my friend. All for Louis. I suppose there had to be some insecurity. She didn't want to take a chance of being mean.

He still was my friend.

My mother always said, "You lose them how you got them."

Which didn't apply to me because I was faithful.

175

I honestly lived my best life, doing what was right, never deliberately hurting anyone.

Up to and including that day I killed Stephanie.

My worst moments were the days and weeks after when I tried to find every excuse as to why I didn't stop, why I plowed through her ... every excuse. Maybe I did so because I had never done anything wrong.

Talk about a spiraling life.

I am glad I didn't die that day because even though I still carry the heavy heartbreaking aftereffects of Stephanie's death, I get to do something good.

End my life making a difference.

Stephanie would never know, her family that loved her would never know.

I would.

They never got justice or peace, but at least for them, I was doing something positive with my second chance at life.

But my conscience wasn't clear. I couldn't go off without telling Stan the truth.

Twice while I was getting ready, he stopped to see me. He was worried, genuinely concerned.

I needed to tell him the truth. I couldn't walk away from him without him knowing that I wasn't some wonderful person and self-sacrificing. Even if he never thought of me the same way again, Stan needed to know.

For the short time I knew him he was good to me.

Stan was with Renee and Nick in what looked like it had been a waiting room at one time. They were there to say goodbye, to watch out the window as we drove off.

I wanted to pull Stan away, just for a moment. Even though Renee knew my history, it was my story to tell him.

He wasn't going to make it easy.

As if we were soldiers going off to war, Stan congratulated each of us.

Renee wished the others luck, not me. A part of me just wanted her to stop. To just be nice before I left, but she was ensuring, in her own way, my conscience wasn't clear.

"And you," Stan put his hand on my cheek. "You look like a man but know I am very proud of you, and I'll tell you again, when you get back."

I reached up and grabbed his hand. "Stan, can we talk?"

"We're talking now."

Renee in her hateful manner, spoke up. "She probably wants you to tell her once more how she's a life saver, a hero." She huffed.

"Okay, alright." Stan stepped back from me and faced her. "That is enough out of you. I have been listening to you and your snide comments to this woman for days. Days. I get you thought she was dead, and you mourned her, blah, blah, blah, that you were pissed she did a Marilyn Monroe, because you felt compelled to bring it up every chance you got. Get over it. Why is this backwards? Shouldn't Viv be bitter at you? Didn't you steal her husband?"

Renee gasped.

I turned to Stan. "It's okay, let it go."

"Tell him that," Renee snapped. "Let him think you're miss perfect. Let me tell you something Stan, that night she tried to take her life wasn't the beginning. It was the end in a long line of shit she put me and Louis through. Dragging us down."

"Oh, she dragged you down?" Stan asked.

I winced. It was not how I wanted him to find out.

"She dragged us down financially and emotionally."

"I don't see how."

"Ha," Renee scoffed. "You have no idea what she put us through! What we went through. No idea because you weren't affected like us. You don't know what she did to make me hate her."

"You don't think?" Stan asked. "If you don't think I didn't know who she was the second I saw her in Bethe's then you're sadly mistaken. I told you my name. None of you paid attention or didn't put two and two together. Stan Miller. Stephanie was my youngest granddaughter and if I am not bitter and angry with her, then you sure as shit have no right to be."

I don't know what happened to me at that moment. My bottom dropped out, I sunk and instead of facing it, I ran. I ran out of that room. Humiliated and wanting to die all over again.

How? How could I do that to him? How many times did Stan wait for me to say something?

Oh God.

"Vivian," Stan called my name.

I kept moving,

"Vivian, I can not catch you. You need to stop."

I did and I slowly turned around.

Stan walked toward me. "I should have said I knew. I should have."

"What?" I said almost gasping. "I should have told you."

"But I knew. I recognized you. How could I not?"

"I didn't recognize you. I figured you and Bess didn't come to the trial because you hated me and couldn't face me."

Stan shook his head. "We didn't go because it was a lynching. Yep, my baby was killed. I hurt. I hurt for my entire family, but it was an accident. It was a mistake. *You* made a mistake. Sending you to jail, telling you how your mistake hurt us ... that wasn't bringing Stephanie back. You didn't have a crime to pay for."

"Stan, I'm sorry. I am so sorry," I sobbed and couldn't stop. "I'm so sorry I did this to you and your family. I am so sorry I hit Stephanie. I live with this, I know this, I will never forget it. But please, please, please know I am so sorry for what I did."

Stan grabbed hold of me and embraced me. "I know you are. I know you are. And if this is the reason you're doing this suicide mission—"

"It's not." I cried harder, allowing him to hold me. "I need to do something good. I really do."

"Hey." Stan spoke gently and broke the embrace. He stared at me. "For what it's worth, please know, Bess and I ... we forgive you. We forgave you a while ago."

I crumbled, emotionally and physically, I crumbled.

Though I was far from forgiving myself, a weight like no other was lifted from me and I felt it.

Stan had said 'For what it's worth', little did he realize his words were worth everything to me at that moment and would be for the rest of my life.

THIRTY-SIX
DAY CAMP

Suddenly, I felt like a different person. I truly did. I had a purpose, and that was to not only find out the information, but to get back to Stan.

To live.

As we pulled away, I saw Stan watching out the window, and I stared back for as long as I could.

It was a late in the day start, in the major told us which exit to get off to find a place to camp out. Somewhere secluded, yet not too far to walk to Nashville.

A small, historic bed and breakfast set off the secondary road and up a long driveway. I had seen a sign stating it was closed until May, which told me there were no bodies.

At least not a lot of bodies.

The bed and breakfast was without power, but it had a working fire place. We wouldn't use it unless it got too cold. With us being so close to Nashville, I didn't want to send up smoke signals.

We brought our own supplies, including a portable stove. Supplies that would last for a week, because that was the time limit we had given ourselves.

Devon was hot and cold with speaking.

Owens said the line, 'what did he say' so much, that I told him to stop, that I would just get into the habit of automatically translating.

We sat on our sleeping rolls on the floor on the parlor, Kate was on watch, then Dan would switch so Owens and I could get rest. We dined on a meal of beef stew with hard, 'Meals Ready to Eat' biscuits. Devon devoured his plate. Scraping the bottom of his dish with the hard biscuit to get every drop of gravy.

I gave him a little more.

It was that scoop of food that turned the tides. He was grateful and he started talking.

"At a walking distance of three hours from base, you will see a bright yellow sun on a green sign. That is where the soldiers go daily to salvage."

It was an odd comment and I told Owens and Dan what he said.

"What in the heck is a yellow sun on a green sign?" Owens asked.

I shrugged.

"Six miles," Dan said. "Average person walks two miles an hour. Three hours from base is about six miles walk."

Owens shook his head. "They're soldiers they move faster."

"Guys, really, I'm more curious as to what and why they are salvaging," I said and asked Devon what they were salvaging and why.

"Things we need," he replied.

"Ask him if it's where we meet the others," Owens said. "And if they'll notice the missing third."

After figuring out how to successfully translate that, I did.

Devon held out his empty plate.

"Oh, come on." Owens snapped and lifted a bottle and took a drink. "How about some of this instead."

Devon reached for it.

"Stop it, he's a kid." I pushed the bottle away and gave Devon a scoop of stew.

As soon as he got his helping, Devon started talking again.

"Wow." I stated after listening shocked, then looked at Owens and Dan. "He said not to talk. They don't talk to each other. They aren't permitted. They must be silent. Follow what the others do. even on base. Their quarters are in room Soap and Satan, but I think he meant Soap and Sudsy. It was probably a store at the mall. He didn't say that last part, I did."

Coughing out a slight, "Ha," Owens sipped his beverage again. "That's really detailed."

"I know," I said. "He must like the stew."

After holding his plate, I gave him another small helping and Devon spoke some more.

"What's he saying now?" Owens asked.

"His quarters are considered level one sector four," I replied. "They will do the bell and call sections for meals, and we are to line up. We'll see the others do it."

"Oni budut delat' pereklichku vo vremya yedy," Devon said

"They'll do roll call at mealtime," I translated.

"Vy dolzhny skazat', chto vy Slavano dva tri chetyre on Osla Odin sem' chetyre."

182

"That's a mouthful," Owens commented.

"He said at roll call we are to say I am Slavano two three four, you are Osla One seven four

"No. No." Owens shook his head. "Too much information. No one likes stew that much."

Dan replied, "Maybe he never had it."

"Ask him why he is telling us all this information. I don't trust it," Owens requested.

I did, I asked.

"It will not work," Devon said in his language.

I held up my hand to Owens and repeated what Devon had told me. Then I asked Devon, "Why won't it work?"

"It just won't. You will get in with ease, but you will never find anything out."

"So why do you want to help us?" I asked. "I mean this is a lot of information."

I heard Owens tell Dan, "I hate when she just starts saying things we don't understand."

"I asked him why he wants to help us." I explained.

"And?" asked Owens.

"He said they're here to save the world. He wants to get to his father. And we can help him." I looked at Devon, "Where is your father. What sector?"

He told me his father was on level three, sector one. I was relieved to hear his father wasn't in the Soap and Sudsy store.

"Don't worry," I reached out patting his hand. "You'll see your father. Unless we aren't back, then they take you back to our base."

His eyes widened and the plate toppled from his hand.

"If you're helping us then don't worry," I said.

Immediately, in a panic, he shook his head, speaking fast, "Net. YA dolzhen vernut'sya cherez pyat' dney. YA dolzhen vernut'sya, ili ya umru."

"That doesn't make sense," I said in English to Owens.

"What? What doesn't make sense? We don't understand him," Owens said.

"He told me he has to be back in five days. He has to be with them," I said, then looking at the visually upset young man. "If he's not ... He says he'll die."

THIRTY-SEVEN
CATCHING UP

The entire night while I tried to sleep, I kept teetering between going with Owens' mistrust and believing the words of a scared teenage boy.

He gave us all that information for a few helpings of stew. But was it all that much?

He knew I spoke the language and I would know right away if he set us up. If Devon was so fearful about not being back in five days, fearful of dying, then he was doing all he could to get back and that meant helping us.

Why would he die?

The only thing I could think of, and Owens agreed, was they were doing another attack in five days. Devon needed to be back at his base to avoid it.

"Are your boots hurting?" Owens asked as we walked. We had been moving about two hours at that point.

"No, why?"

"You're slowing."

"No, I just can't keep up with your big steps. If you would take normal strides."

"I am taking normal strides."

I scoffed.

"Do you need to stop again?" Owens asked.

185

"I didn't need to stop last time, that was you. Now can we continue."

"Fine," Owens huffed.

"Say it."

"Odin…"

"Nope."

"Is it Odin as in Thor?" Owens asked.

"Sort of but not Oh … more like Uh."

"Okay," Owes said. "Osla … Odin … shitter."

"What?" I laughed.

"That's what you said."

"No, it isn't. It's chit-tear."

"I'm not hearing it."

"You've practiced that one line for hours. You keep messing it up. Is it a mental block?"

"Maybe, I don't know." Owens shrugged.

"You say it like that, it's gonna be a sure sign we aren't part of them," I told him.

"I got news for you, the moment we say it, perfect or not, they're putting us in the firing squad. It's a set up."

"It's a number."

"It's a set up," Owens repeated. "Like it's the code number for traitor among us. You'll see. What made you choose Russian anyhow?"

"My mother had that mindset like Stan."

"Wait, you said she was a preacher."

"A minister, yeah. She was hardcore."

"What do you mean?" he asked.

"Like all the extreme parts of the bible, she seemed to find as rules to love by."

"So, she hated the Russians?" Owens questioned.

"I think she just mistrusted them and so to irritate her, I learned Russian. Good thing for us. I almost learned Swahili."

"Did she ever say you wouldn't use it?"

I shook my head. "Once I picked Russian she wouldn't let me quit. She had a family in the church take on a Russian exchange student and I was like two years into learning it, by the end of that summer, I was pretty fluent. She thought I was going to be arrested as a spy."

"That's funny."

"I know."

"You should have joined the Army," Owens said.

"Were you married?" I asked.

"No."

"I take it you didn't have kids then."

"That's your mother coming out in you," Owens said. "You can have kids without being married."

"So, you have kids?"

"No."

I grunted.

"You?" he asked.

"No. None."

"Is that why your husband left you for the barely legal hot chick."

"Oh my God." I stopped walking. "How old do you think I am. I can still have children for a lot of years." I started walking again.

"Sorry, I didn't mean to imply, you're old, you just... you know look rough."

"Rough?"

"Yeah, like ... never mind."

"No wonder no one ever married you." I shook my head. "No, I actually had a bad year."

"So, I gathered. I'm sorry about that."

"That was sensitive."

"I can be."

"Hmm." I stopped walking again. "Do you really think Renee is hot."

"Yeah, she is. Young. Is she old enough to drink?"

That made me laugh and I continued to follow him. "I actually asked Louis that. She's like twenty-four."

"Same age as Kate," Owens said.

"And no, he didn't leave me for her to have babies. I wanted kids, I really did, but he couldn't have them. I don't know why he left me for her. Maybe because she was just hot."

"Guys stray for the oddest reasons." This time it was Owens that stopped. "Sunshine."

"What are you talking about?"

Owens pointed to the tall sign. Tall enough to be seen from the highway. It had a green background and a yellow sun, just like Devon said.

It was the JP Oil logo and we had found them.

The moment we knew we had arrived where the soldiers were located, we left the highway. We slipped through the grass, staying low and out of sight until we could blend in.

It was silent. There was no talking, no voices in a quiet world flowing our way. Just footsteps and sounds of rummaging.

Including the JP station, there were three other gas stations, several fast-food places, and a hotel.

One single dump truck was located in the middle of the street.

Binoculars were not part of the uniform, so I knew that after we looked, we had to leave them behind.

"Can you see?" I asked.

"Fucking strange."

"What?"

"Look." He handed me the binoculars. "They aren't carrying more than one item."

At the back of the dump truck stood two uniformed soldiers, their uniforms slightly different and not so storm trooper and tactical.

I watched a line of the grunts approach these men, each showing the item that had. The first four were approved with a nod and the item was placed in the truck. Three were denied and the item they carried discarded in a pile off to the side of the road.

"What are they getting?" I returned the binoculars.

"Wait. The one has a package of twinkies."

"For real?"

"Yeah. He's walking to the truck …accepted."

"They're salvaging junk food?" I questioned.

"I don't think they know exactly what they're salvaging. They're going into the stores, the restaurants and just grabbing."

"It doesn't make sense."

"Neither does Olga Odin Shitter."

"Dude, that's not it."

Owens smiled. "I know what it is. You ready for this?"

I took a deep breath. "I'm ready."

We both lowered our face shields and like everyone else, became just a number.

THIRTY-EIGHT
NOT YOU

The last thing Owens said to me before we separated was to be alert. We never moved far, but no one really paired off so we couldn't either.

I watched what the others did, how they walked, what they did when they went into the stores.

They moved stoically and acted it. Never giving away if they were confused or confident. I wondered if they were real, if perhaps some of them were robotic.

Both Owens and I stayed close to the Rise and Fill Convenience store crew. It had one of those chain coffee places inside, and we moved like they did. Head high, back straight and slow.

They'd walk in, go to the candy aisle, grab one box and walked out, holding it as if it were some great mystery.

I watched one soldier stand before the darkened coolers. Head tilted, he just stood there looking at the soda pop.

Did he even know what to do?

I walked over two cooler doors from him and did the same. Stood there, staring. Then I made the first move, opening the cooler and taking out a single can of Coke.

Holding it like the others held their contribution, I walked out. As I hit the entrance, it had to be Owens that hurried and grabbed a pack of gum.

He did so unlike everyone else and obvious he was trying to catch up to me.

I wanted to yell at him, but I didn't.

Keeping my composure, I walked to the line. There seemed to be a distance of three feet between everyone, and I kept that distance.

But I watched. Watched as a person approached what I called the Leader or Office Soldiers, lifted the object and were told 'yes or no' with a nod.

My turn.

I lifted the soda can, and like the others, didn't move. He was different than the others, a variation in his uniform that screamed to me that actually was one of the big dogs. A silver circle graced his lapel and was the only one that looked like he wore a black turtleneck, instead of a tee shirt, under his cover jacket. I wasn't sure if it was my imagination or not, but the Silver Circle Officer stared at me for the longest time. It seemed he looked at me and not my can.

I dismissed it as my paranoia when he shook his head no.

Turning, I did as the soldier in front of me did and dropped the can in the disposal pile and walked back to the store. Passing Owens, I was a bit annoyed that his single pack of gum was chosen.

It didn't take long to get into the swing of things, and dare I say I was a pro in no time. But it was rather tedious and slow.

Were these officers or leaders idiots making the soldiers salvage one item at a time or were they having them stay busy, like an exercise in patience?

I didn't understand the reasoning and I doubted the soldiers did.

We were at it for hours, no break, when finally, a single blast of an air horn sounded off.

Almost robotically, everyone instantly stopped what they were doing and walked outside.

A new pile had formed by the back of the truck. Stacks of black bottles.

Each soldier walked to the pile and grabbed a bottle without pausing and without looking. They then formed two lines on opposite sides of the truck.

I did the same, the bottle was heavy and as I moved it, it sounded like liquid. No one drank. I would wait until I saw someone else open the bottle.

The silver circle officer looked at me again, but this time with a pause as he made his way to the driver's seat..

I tried not to make eye contact and I wanted badly to find Owens to see if he noticed it.

It wasn't my imagination. Did he know something? If so, why didn't he say anything.

Maybe he would.

I would find out soon enough if it was going to be the shortest infiltration attempt in history.

The truck began to move slowly and the two lines of soldiers on both sides followed diligently.

More than likely we were headed back to base. The sun was setting, and at the painfully slow pace that we moved, it surely would be dark when we arrived.

Owens was wrong. Yes, they were soldiers, but they didn't move fast. On the other hand, everything Devon had told us was correct. I had no doubt the rest of the information would be just as accurate.

The power was out, and the exterior of the abandoned mall was dark and apocalyptic, but as we neared the entrance, I could see it was lit inside.

The truck turned in the parking lot and the line of soldiers kept moving to the doors.

I was worried. I knew we were level one, but what was sector four?

It was the single moment I worried I would expose our cover.

But unexpectedly, everything changed once we walked in.

The soldiers in black relaxed, they separated, going off on their own. No longer following a strict line.

We entered by an abandoned JC Penny's. There were two levels above us. I glanced up and saw a couple of those officer uniforms. The interior was lit by spotlights and the sound of the generators hummed.

Sector Four, I thought and just moved hoping not to mosey around the mall looking for the Soap and Sudsy store like I was a browsing Christmas shopper.

Even though the others relaxed, it was apparent they still knew where they were going.

Then just after the empty water fountain near the escalator, I spotted the familiar logo of the Soap and Sudsy. I pivoted right, hoping Owens was following me and I slowed down my pace.

Trying not to be obvious, I peered in each room as I passed it, I could hear talking, low voices.

Inside, they conversed.

I picked up bits and pieces of things they said.

My first thought was 'shit' when we arrived at the Soap and Sudsy.

Owens and I were not alone.

There were six floor mats on the floor made up perfectly as beds.

A lantern was between them.

One soldier sat on the mat reading a book, his mask down as if it were so normal to read with the face covered.

I knew I wasn't going to get a chance to tell Owens anything and we were out of our element.

I didn't even know where we went to the bathroom or which floor mat was mine.

It was also the first I saw someone open the black bottle. A soldier entered our room and opened it immediately, downing the beverage.

I made eye contact with Owens. It was at that precise moment when I wondered what the hell we were thinking, the alarm blasted. Two short blasts then a third.

Book Soldier immediately stood, the other put down his bottle and both hurried out of the Soap and Sudsy. It was the fastest I had seen any of them move.

Owens and I followed suit.

If Devon was right, it was the dinnertime line-up.

They stood at ease, hands behind back in one long row.

There were hundreds of us.

Admittedly, I was hungry and curious as to what we would be served.

One of the leader soldiers started at the end of the line to my right. Down by the Victoria Secrets.

I was confident as the leader walked by each soldier and each soldier gave a rendition of what Devon told us to say.

They said their name and number and the leader kept walking.

I thought, 'please, Owens do this right.' Book Soldier was between us.

The leader neared Owens. I waited and closed my eyes, hoping for the best.

Then he arrived at Owens.

"Olga ... Oh-den ... Shit-tear."

FUCK!

It was so bad, anyone could tell he didn't have a clue about dialect.

But the leader kept going and I breathed out in relief.

Book Soldier gave his name and number, then me.

I deepened my voice and spoke with perfection, "Slavano dva tri chetyre."

The leader took a step.

From above, a booming voice echoed to us, bouncing off the empty galleys of the mall and bringing an instantaneous halt to everything.

"Ostanovka!" he hollered for the leader to stop. "Ver-nites' nazad i voz'mite etogo soldata."

I cringed.

He had told the leader to back up and 'get that soldier'. I knew he meant Owens and his hick version of a Russian language.

I cursed and swore under my breath as the leader moved to Owens. I raised my eyes trying not to move my head, trying to see who was calling the orders.

Then the same voice called out. "Ne on. Von tot."

Not him. That one.

And before I knew it, they weren't grabbing Owens, they were taking me.

I could feel and sense the concern and panic coming from Owens as a different leader soldier came for me.

He was a professional, he would stay the course.

He knew we had Devon. At the very least I would find Devon's father and maybe use that to my advantage.

I was brought to the top level and to the very end past the food courts, where the tables were packed with soldiers eating their meals.

Their masks off, they looked normal. Some as young as Devon.

Surprisingly, I wasn't nervous. I was led down a long hall to an office at the end.

A security office and standing there was the Silver Circle Officer from salvaging.

He told the other leader to leave us and close the door.

I just stood there.

When the door shut, he walked around and stood before me, staring at me for a second.

"Umnaya," he said. Which meant 'Clever'. Then he stated what I thought should have been obvious to me. "No u nas net zhenshchin."

'We have no women.'

With that, he lifted my mask.

He was nearly breathless for at least a few seconds staring at me. Then he removed his facial covering. He was not as old as I thought he'd be. His husky voice was misleading, and he was a man in his mid-thirties.

He stepped closer and spoke in perfect English. "Where … is my son?"

THRITY-NINE
SAVE THE WORLD

To say I was a plethora of questions was an understatement. They ranged from where they were from, what they were doing in the US, why they attacked, and I wasn't buying that radical 'save the world' crap either.

The first question that popped in my mind was why this officer guy kept staring at me.

Even after we moved to a meeting room on the same floor.

Staring.

He'd take a few steps, stop, look at me, and repeat.

"Are you hungry?" he asked.

"Not yet," I answered. "Look, I know you said you don't have women."

"Not in the service and not many outside of it."

"I get it, but can you stop staring at me. It's rude and you're looking at me like I'm an anomaly."

"You *are* an anomaly."

"Okay. Great. Stop staring."

"Yes." He nodded and took a seat.

"What is your name?" I asked.

"You can call me Miller."

Hearing it stumbled me emotionally, it was odd and a strange coincidence. Was it some sort of sign from Stan. "Just Miller?"

"Yes, for now. I know you are not alone. I know you have a lot of questions. Would you like your partner here?"

"I know you aren't going to kill me."

He shook his head. "No."

"Are you going to kill my partner?"

"No."

"Do you think I need him for protection because I'm a woman?"

He laughed.

"What is so funny?"

"Nothing." Miller waved out his hand. "Just tell me who he is. I'm torn between two."

Now, it was my turn to laugh. "You really …. Really don't know?"

He shook his head.

"How can you not know?"

"It's tough. You, it was easy. I sent for all three," he said. "Three?"

"The ones in your sleeping room. I figured he was one of them."

Within seconds there was a knock at the door and an escort soldier brought in Owens and two others. I knew one was Owens right away because he was taller.

The escort soldier also handed a long black case to Miller.

Miller went back to speaking Russian and thanked the escort for the men and the case which he put on the meeting table.

He requested the three soldier for their 'call numbers'. And as we did lining up for meals, they each gave their number with Owens, badly stating his, "Olga … Oh-den … shitter."

The jig was up and Miller walked over to the men, but to my surprise he lifted the mask of the middle soldier, not Owens.

"Are you serious, right now?" I blasted. "That is not him. Are you dense?"

The recently unmasked soldier looked mortified when I said that. Not that he understood me, I didn't think he did, but probably my tone.

"Him." I walked up to Owens. "This is him." I lifted his mask.

"Viv!" Owens blasted. "What the fuck. You just gave me up."

"Like he wouldn't know."

"I take back what I said that you should have joined the Army," Owens said.

Miller dismissed the two soldiers and escort then shut the door.

"How did you not know it was him?" I asked. "He speaks the language so badly."

"Why are you speaking English to him?" Owens questioned.

Miller responded. "We have several that don't speak well."

Owens looked at him. "Okay why is he speaking perfect English now too."

"Because he can," I replied.

"Both of you please sit down." Miller looked at Owens, doing that staring thing at him.

Owens sat down next to me. "Why is he staring."

"He does that, it's weird."

"I'm sorry." Miller waved out his hand. "Now this case has proof."

"Proof of what?" I asked.

"Of what I am going to tell you."

Owens shook his head. "If it's some outlandish militia stuff. There's no proof."

"No," Miller said slightly exasperated. "You'll see. And it is good faith for the exchange."

"Exchange what?" I asked.

"I know you want answers and I want my son," he said.

"Who is your son?" I questioned.

"You're wearing his uniform."

"Ah, Devon. He's very nice and very scared."

"He's not really a soldier but I wasn't leaving him behind," Miller said.

"That's how you knew," I said. "You knew by the uniform."

"That and you used the code number for infiltrator."

"Ha!" Owens blasted. "I told you. I told you."

"You did."

Owens smiled in a smug way then turned serious. "Wait. Why is this not feeling like an interrogation."

"It's not," Miller said. "We don't need information from you. We don't want to kill you."

I scoffed. "You killed billions."

"We did. They were already dead."

Owens shook his head. "No, they weren't. We watched the CCTV. We watched people just drop dead, cars crash. They weren't already dead."

"Yes, they were. They just didn't know it yet."

"What kind of bull shit is that?" asked Owens.

Miller snapped open the case. "Before our arrival. There were eight billion people on the planet, correct." He opened the case and turned it to us.

The lid was a long screen, black and nothing on it.

Below it looked like a keyboard and black box with a green light.

Miller rolled his chair over to be next to me and share the view. "We worked hard on this presentation," he said. "We had it just in case you ... just in case we needed to say what was going on."

"You attacked and invaded us," I said. "We want to know but in reality, you don't have to tell us anything."

"Yes we do. We did it also so going forward someone would know." He clicked a few buttons on the keyboard and an image of a wildfire appeared. "It's no secret to you that wildfires had increased by seventy percent before our presence was here. This past winter of this year, fourteen winter wildfires. They are rare. Once a decade. Fourteen in one winter."

"Oh, good Lord," Owens chimed in. "Really, you destroyed the world because we already destroyed it. Your organization are climate nut jobs."

"Hey," I snapped. "That shit is real."

Miller looked at me. "It's an ongoing argument. You'll learn to ignore it."

"What do you mean?" I asked.

"Let me continue. To your knowledge there are two main wildfire seasons a year," he said. "Spring and early fall. Imagine it being a constant thing."

Owens looked at me. "This is why they ended the world. Who are you people?"

Miller ignored his question and changed the image. It was a city ablaze. An entire city.

"On September twenty-eight of this year, Los Angeles burns to the ground. Too big to stop, to put out. It burns it spreads and for thirty days, countless cities are reduced to ashes, millions homeless. Tens of thousands are dead and it's just the start...."

"Stop." I held up my hand. "September of this year? It's only April."

Miller continued, "By January ..." he changed the image. That one was the ruins of Los Angeles buried in ice and snow. "The cloud still hadn't cleared, causing a mini ice age in the region, and forcing a mass exodus of ninety percent of California."

I watched the pictures scroll by, one by one. Different places, different fires, snow.

People living in camps.

"But the exodus didn't help," he continued. "Because it was everywhere. Most was concentrated here in the United States, but everywhere. Nobody was ready, despite expert warning. And the grand famine began ... Riots started as well. I'm not sure what started the entire nuclear conflict, but that was it. Illness raged, no food, mankind on its last—"

Owens silenced him with one short, sharp, loud whistled.

I put my finger to my ear. "Ow that hurt."

"Hold it. Stop." Owens formed a T with his hands. "None of this happened."

"It will. It's started already, you know it, but the big ball starts rolling in September and it doesn't stop," Miller explained. "Within four years the population in the US alone is cut in half, another three years, chaos, gangs, violence, disease leaves maybe twenty percent."

"Again ..." Owens said loudly. "You need to stop. Call me stupid but ..."

"I would never." Miller said seriously.

I laughed.

"Why is this funny?" Owens looked at me.

"It's not," I told him. "Just when did the lightbulb go off."

"Viv," Owens said. "It's not possible. He's implying they're from the future."

"Thirty-seven years," Miller said.

Owens shook his head. "It's a lie."

"Then explain the photograph slides," Miller stated.

"Photo shop." Owens nodded.

"And our weapon?"

After a quick glance to me, Owens replied. "The Russians."

"Okay, I'll give you that," Miller agreed. "They had the technology or the basis for it. It was pushed forward and developed the same time the plan to come back was hatched."

"Time travel is not possible," Owens said.

"Right now. It's not. The tools are there. It took one missing scout in our time who disappeared and returned to confirm what science has been speculating for years," Miller said. "And the process, once we realized how, took fifteen years. We nailed it. As you can tell. We're here."

"Then how?" Owens asked. "Did someone build a machine. Aliens?"

Miller shook his head. "No, the ability has always been here. There are these areas of great electromagnetic force."

I knew exactly what he was talking about. "The twelve Vile Vortices."

"Yes." Miller nodded and gave me this closed mouth smile.

"What the hell are they?" Owens asked.

"Twelve spots across the globe," I explained. "Where it's proven that vortexes of increased electromagnetic fields are present. Bermuda triangle is the most famous. I began my obsession with them since the Captain Emery claim."

"The Emery Claim," Owens said in disbelief.

"Captain Emery disappeared in the Antarctic on fly over expedition and reappeared six years later in the Bermuda triangle. It was a blip in time to him," I replied. "A man named Ivan Sanderson spent his life studying it."

Miller wagged his finger. "An old book of his was actually the key to harnessing it."

"Which one?" I asked.

"Please, both of you stop. Let's assume .." Owens said. "All of this is true. So the plan was come back and kill everyone? How is that saving the world?"

"As I said, the population is decreased by eighty percent in seven years," Miller answered. "There are no resources because mankind and the nuclear war just destroyed them. Salvaging for what remains is heartbreaking."

I interjected because I got it. I got what he was saying. "You jumpstarted it."

"What?" Owens asked.

"They jumpstarted it," I explained. "It was a slow burn. Half the population died, and the other half not only used all the resources, they destroyed them. There was no future. No way to survive long term. So, instead of waiting for it. They wiped out eighty percent now to preserve the planet, stop the nuclear war and give the future a chance."

With an excited slam of his hand to the table, Miller chuckled. "That is absolutely right. But we settled on seventy-five percent."

Owens grumbled sarcastically. "Very generous."

Miller smiled. "Thank you. We figured even at seventy-five percent gone, it's still more people than three hundred years ago. We didn't evenly distribute, in low risk, low war areas, we left a higher percentage alive. The entire plan took nearly twenty-five years from concept to finish."

"I understand," I said. "I really do. But it's not only ambitious, it's a little insane. Who came up with this plan? You? No, wait, you're not old enough. It's not you."

He shook his head. "No, it is not."

"Then who?" I asked.

Miller looked directly at me. "You."

FORTY
LIFE IN FIFTEEN MINUTES

No.

That was my first thought. My second thought was that it was a joke. That was one I quickly dismissed when I realized Miller didn't really joke around.

The moment Owens said, "I don't know why, but after listening to this conversation, that actually makes sense."

I followed that with, "I need a drink."

Miller stood. "I figured you'd say that." And he excused himself from the room.

After he left, for whatever reason, I looked at Owens. "Why did you say it made sense."

"You knew about the twelve whatever things," he said. "And the reason just clicked for you. Only someone that is on that mindset could think of it."

"I don't understand. He said he came from thirty-seven years in the future. Right?"

Owens nodded.

"I was dead. I killed myself. Aberdeen said that the pulse acted opposite on those who had recently died. Like me, Nash, Stan … If it wasn't for the Pulse, I would have died. I would have been dead."

I had been so engrossed in that few seconds talking to Owens, I didn't know that Miller had been standing in the door.

"That's not true. You didn't die." He set a bottle on the table. It was an odd-shaped round bottle like nothing I had ever seen. The body of the bottle was carved wood. He placed a glass down. "Have your drink. I brought it because I knew you'd say that, you know, if we ran into you. I'm sorry I didn't have it ready." He pushed a glass forward and poured about a shot's worth of liquid in the glass. It was cloudy and slightly brown.

"What is it?" I asked.

"Your favorite. We make it. Your ... drink of choice," Miller said. "Can I ... can I ask where my son is."

"He's fine," I replied, lifting the glass. "He isn't that far from here. I wouldn't hurt him."

"I didn't think you would."

I sniffed the beverage, it didn't really have a strong scent. With a shrug, I took a gulp. At first it kind of tasted like oats, then as it hit my throat rolling into my esophagus, I felt it.

It should have been called fire water, it was so strong and burning, for an instant, I thought he was poisoning me. My glands salivated.

"Oh ... My ... God!" I gasped out. "Holy shit." I twitched my head a couple times trying to shake it.

"That strong?" Owens asked.

"You tell me." I slid the glass to him, and his reaction was nearly the same as mine.

"You drink that stuff?" Owens asked Miller.

Miller pointed at me. "She does. Like water."

209

"Really?" I asked surprised. "I must be tough."

"That's an understatement."

"Wow, do I become like Sarah Connor?" I questioned.

"Bet you do," Owens said.

"Who?" Miller asked.

"Never mind. But ... am I like all muscular? Sarah was badass buff even as she got older."

"No," he said courtly. "You drink too much to work out."

With a shrug and a tilt of my head, I refreshed the glass and brought it to my lips.

Owens gave a quirky look. "I thought that was too strong."

"Look. If my seventy-four-year-old self can handle this, I can handle it." I took another sip. It actually went down easier.

"Now that you're in a solid state of mind," Miller said.

Owens chuckled out, "What? Drinking is her solid state of mind?"

"She is less emotional." Miller looked at me. "You didn't die that night. I mean technically you did. The weapon didn't bring you back, the paramedics did. Your husband at the time had induced vomiting and you were told you died when he was getting a rag to clean you up. It's a well known story. You tell it a lot."

I sat back. "I brag about trying to take my life?"

"Not bragging, teaching," Miller answered. "You attempted to die two days before your sentencing hearing. That was delayed but not cancelled. It was ... it was as if your attempt at suicide was a way to try to gain sympathy."

"It wasn't."

"I know, but that is what you say people thought," Miller continued. "You were sentenced to ten years. You didn't appeal. You went to prison. Your friends all abandoned you …"

"I have news for you. They abandoned me long before that sentencing hearing."

"Well, anyone who remained … left. Louis got married and moved."

"That sucks," Owens commented. "I mean I guess they weren't friends to begin with."

"I tell myself that," I replied.

"Not everyone abandoned you," Miller said. "Those you knew. But one guy became your friend. He said he had a near death experience and was told not to abandon you."

"Stan," I whispered his name.

Miller nodded. "Stan. He had that heart attack, survived it and visited you three times a week for years. Your imprisonment sheltered you from the fires that brought chaos and starvation. Prison got tough, food scarce, but you had this keen foresight to stockpile. You accredited it to Stan. It was very hard when he died. Fortunately, as you always said, it only a month before the nuclear confrontation. He didn't have to live through that. The prison system broke down, the guards freed everyone. But you stayed."

"I … stayed in jail?" I questioned in disbelief.

"You did," Miller answered. "You didn't know what was out there. If it was safe, dangerous. You and fourteen others stayed behind. Five months. You survived by —"

"Please don't tell me I ate people."

211

Miller laughed. "No. You had stockpiled and gathered what remained. All but four of the fourteen died. You probably would have stayed there longer, good thing for us that you didn't."

"What made me leave?" I asked.

Miller pointed to Owens.

"Him?"

"Me?"

"Yes. He and three others were salvaging. They found you and the others. It was a rescue, but not how you think. He and the three others were starving. Two of his men needed medical attention. And that was why you left. To get it. You didn't want to watch another person die. But at that point international help had landed or invaded and the Russian Army had ground forces. You communicated and got them help."

"I stayed with the Russian Army, didn't I?" I asked.

"You did. Because you felt it was your way to help. But it was a long road and the land was too toxic. You and a few hundred others left with the troops and returned to Russian. Things didn't get better, actually, worse everywhere as you know. The safest place to go was north. Siberia. You helped a Russian General mobilize a survival pilgrimage. Scientists, doctors, soldiers, civilians. I was born in Siberia. The first baby born there. Within a month of arriving. We were living, growing, the air was good, but we knew time was limited. We had some really good scientists. It was a farmer that went scouting that sparked the idea of the vortexes. He disappeared and came back saying he was in the future, and no one was there. We still don't know how he managed to make it back."

"In Siberia?" I asked. "There's none in Siberia."

"Yes, there is. That's how you came up with the idea of a do over. They worked on using the Vortex to go back. Armies were built and trained, and the weapon was constructed. It was a race against extinction because we were not only starving but a virus killed off most of the women. We haven't had a child born in ten years.."

"Holy shit," Owens exclaimed. "So, when did she leave the US before or after population dropped to twenty percent."

"Before. By the time the world started dying off, we were in Siberia."

Owens lifted his hand. "I might be wrong, but according to Back to the Future, she really shouldn't know too much of her future, right?"

Miller shook his head. "It's a totally different path now. Eighty-five percent of all wildfires are started by humans. No humans, most of the destructive wildfires won't happen. No humans, no chaos, no war."

"What about that chick virus?" Owens asked.

"We cured it. We're ready for it," Miller said. "But that won't be for some time. If it happens."

"Could be a Siberia thing," I said. "We were cut off from the world. Did we ever send scouts south? Did we try to make contact?"

"We did. We tried reaching out, sending troops. The world around us died. We were pretty much that remained."

"How did you know when to do the Pulse or whatever you call the weapon?" I asked.

"The scrambler. Bad name, I know. We chose the time we knew we could save you. We knew it had the opposite effect on those who recently died. So we picked the day that you died. We immediately went to look for you, but you were gone."

Owens whistled. "I lucked out. I could have died."

"No." Miller shook his head. 'We sent that message to your phone telling you to get back to base. Our whole entire base of operations was this area because we wanted to be around where both of you were."

I was full of questions, even more than when Miller started explaining. I was sure I'd get the answers.

But oddly he talked about me and my life. My entire life, yet to be lived, delivered to me like a Wikipedia synopsis in less than fifteen minutes. But how did Miller know so many details.

"How do you know so much about me?" I asked. "Are we close."

"I should hope," Miller replied. "I'm your son."

FORTY-ONE
TRUTH UNFOLDS

Resisting the urge to turn in my chair and snap at Owens that I told him I wasn't too old to have a child, I just stared at Miller, trying to find some resemblance to me.

I didn't see it.

But the name.

Miller.

"I named you after Stan?" I asked.

"Yes. Miller is my first name, Stanly is my middle name. Are you sure you are not hungry? It's well past dinner time and you tend to get upset easily when you are hungry."

"Thought you said drinking helped," Owens said.

"I did."

"You're my son," I stated. "Like flesh and blood son or did I just assume you."

Owens laughed. "Assumed. That's funny."

"No, you carried me," Miller replied. "You trekked into Siberia eight months pregnant."

"Wow. Now ... does Devon know me."

"Of course, he adores you," Miller replied.

"That's weird. He didn't say anything."

"Would you believe him?" Miller asked. "No."

"Plus," Owens said. "He probably didn't recognize you. You're a lot bigger in the future."

"What?" I turned to him. "What does that mean? Why would you say that?"

He pointed at Miller. "He said you don't exercise."

"He said I don't work out," I snapped. "He didn't say I was fat." I then turned to Miller. "Am my heavy in the future?"

"No. No." Miller shook his head. "Thick."

"Thick? I'm thick?"

Holding up his hand, Miller tried to calm me. "You need to eat. Can we just continue. I know it's late, I won't get to Devon tonight. But I would like to get him first thing."

"Yeah." I nodded. "But before we go on, is there *any*thing else you want to tell me that will just throw me through a loop?"

"Um …" Miller pursed his lips. "Not that I can think of."

"Good," Owens said. "Can we move on from her biography and ask questions?"

"Sure, please." Miller held out his hand.

"How many of you came through?" Owens asked.

"Everyone. Every person in our city. Which isn't many. Seventeen hundred and three. We had some stay back, several to man the device that captures the energy to put us through."

"I stayed behind, didn't I?" I asked.

"You did," Miller replied. "You and my father and most of the older generation did. We did several test trips. Each time we were able to return to the exact same spot."

With huff through his nostrils, Owens shook his head. "How did you emerge in this time in Siberia and not get shot trudging through Russia."

"You guys said the same thing during planning. Ships. Two. One to man the vortex, the other for us to go through. An old cruise ship. Without getting into technicalities, we devised a way to create our own fuel and retrofitted old trucks. We pilgrimed back down to meet the ships. It was an empty overgrown world and hard to travel. We did it. Obviously. We allowed enough time so we didn't miss the window for your death. After we arrived, I came ahead with a team of ten, crossing the border and coming to this mall to wait it out. Then after we detonated the weapon from the ship, the soldiers came."

"Did I devise the whole mad plan?" I asked.

"Most of it." Miller nodded. "The hard decisions, like where to eliminate the most people, where to save. Including luring some of the planes to land to get women. Just very detailed, I brought your notebooks. You wrote in one constantly."

Owens asked, "How did you just detonate a weapon and not erase yourself? I mean, obviously you saved your mother. What if you inadvertently killed a grandparent or parent."

"That was a risk and gamble we took," Miller said. "Most of us here were born in the post war world. With eighty percent gone, it was a safe gamble that we wouldn't kill our lineage. We did lose people. Thirty. And there are at least two dozen who look totally different now. We did go to lengths to make sure some people survived."

"What about my husband?" I asked. "I'm sure he was in Russia."

Miller chuckled. "No, you know he's from here. Please."

When his smile fell from his face upon the revelation that I possible didn't know my future husband, that was when it hit me.

I didn't see the resemblance to me, but I sure as hell suddenly saw it to Owens. My eye shifted from Miller to Owens; they looked too much alike.

"No," I graveled. "He's your father?" I pointed at Owens. "I'm your father?"

"I ... I ..." Miller stammered his words. "I thought you would know. I thought ..."

"No!" I shouted. "I didn't know. You said no more surprises. You said there was nothing left to throw me through a loop!"

Miller stood.

"Where are you going?" I asked.

"To get you food. I'll be back." He walked to the door. "And please make her have another drink."

When he left, Owens poured some into the glass and pushed it my way. "Hey," he said. "At least it won't be a lonely apocalypse."

I snatched up the glass and gulped it in one swallow. It went down easier than the first drink. It also went down easier than the news that I was some genocidal maniac and Owens was the future father of my unborn militant child.

FORTY-TWO
ONCE MORE

It was no wonder Devon tore up that beef stew.

The food they served was in packets, their version of MRE's, but strange.

We ate dried fish, and I made a mental note that should I ever lead the world, we wouldn't be eating dried fish.

The booze left me loopy, and I fell asleep early. I was the first one up and realized they didn't have coffee.

It was close though. A warm cloved beverage that jolted me with energy.

With a barley breakfast bar in hand, we left the mall.

It was different. Although we still wore the uniforms we didn't wear the headgear, and everyone paused to look at us as we walked by.

We picked up a vehicle from a local store parking lot, it would be a lot faster getting back to the bed and breakfast if we drove.

"So, what is up with the slow, one item at a time, salvaging thing," Owens asked. "Surely, that wasn't her idea."

"It's tedious," replied Miller as we drove. "But it is a way to eat up time so to speak. We'll pick up the pace on that once we get our people off the ship."

"Off?" Owens asked. "I thought you'd get back on and go back. That's why your gathering supplies."

"No," Miller told him. "This is our world now. We're staying. The supplies are for now. It will be plentiful. There's a lot of work. Prepare the land for farming, clear the bodies. And with the women, hopefully, we can repopulate. Hopefully. It was so nice to see children. It'll also be nice watching my mother grow old again."

"And yourself being born," Owens said.

"You'll meet Stan," I told him. "Your namesake."

"Yes. But keep in mind. We won't be integrating with the survivors. Not sure after we acclimate to this world, how they will handle us. One thing for sure. It will be a better world."

I asked, "Where are the women now?"

"At a large building near the airport called The Marriott."

Because we knew Dan or Kate would be keeping watch, Owens stopped at the end of the driveway and walked to alert them, he carried the case.

I hung back with Miller.

The plan was he'd get his son, my grandson, and Owens had the honors of informing Dan and Kate what was happening and show them the black case.

A case I presumed we'd take back to Fort Knox.

Once Owens signaled it was clear, we moved forward.

"This is a wonderful building," Miller said. "I really like it."

"It works. Devon is inside. He's not in uniform," I told him. "He has blue jeans on. Why does he not speak English?"

"He does. Everyone does. You have orders for no one to speak English or let on they understand. When people think you don't know what you're saying, they tend to say a lot."

When we arrived at the front door, Devon came blasting out.

He paused on the last step, then flew to his father.

Owens lifted the case. "I'll uh go tell Dan and Kate the future stuff."

I nodded, then faced Miller and Devon as they reunited.

"It's okay," Miller said to Devon. "You can speak English. She knows."

Devon backed from the embrace, then hugged me. "Babka," he said warmly.

I returned the hug, wondering if the reason I felt a closeness to Devon the whole time was because of the connection.

"What now?" I asked Miller as I ended the hug with Devon. "We only discussed to this point. Are you going with us to Fort Knox?"

"No. We have work to do. We planned that if and when we located you, we would have you and my father with us. And now this Dan and Kate because they know."

"We have to go back to Fort Knox, to Aberdeen and Stan. Should we keep the case or bring it back to you?" I asked.

"You can't tell an entire base what has happened, you can't," Miller said. "Especially not right now. You know as well as I do many military survived, they will launch an immediate counter strike, especially if they know where we are. There aren't enough of us to defend. We aren't soldiers like my father. We don't have the weapons or ammunition to rage a battle."

"You have weapons, and they perceive you as a threat," I said. "I mean, I perceived you as a threat. You shot my friend."

"We shoot no one without reason. If we shot him, we perceived *him* to be a threat. Our weapon is the long distance Scrambler and miniature which works in areas of a hundred feet. Our goal and plan is to peacefully live here and move on."

"Then I'll find you. I will," I said.

Miller nodded. "You need to do so within four days."

"Four days?" I asked. "You know Devon here was really scared that he would die in five days. That was yesterday."

"As well as he should be. He would be out here without knowledge or protection. He needs to be where he can be kept safe."

"Safe? Safe from what?" I questioned.

"Mama." He placed his hands on my shoulders. "It's not done. The scrambler will be recharged in four days. We need to finish what we started. We're only at fifty-five, sixty percent."

I gasped and stumbled back. "You're detonating the weapon again."

"Yes. It's the plan," he said. "Your plan."

FORTY-THREE
DECISIONS

My plan? My plan? I was truly a madman in the future.

What made me into such a monster that I thought killing people was a great idea. Killing them in a snap, like the Marvel villain, Thanos.

My God I was like Thanos, I believed I was doing it for the good of mankind.

Miller saw it on my face, I know he did. He asked Devon to give us a moment, and the young man went back inside.

"What is it?" he asked.

"You can't do that. Set the weapon off again. That's a billion people. A billion more people."

"A billion more people that can do damage. That can and will destroy this earth."

"We don't know that."

"Actually, Mama, we spent a lot of time doing the math. Doing the calculations. This wasn't an easy decision for you, but it came down to recreating the loss of eight years into eight minutes."

It was disturbing to me. Just thinking about all the dead bodies I had seen, all of them and it was my doing. "It's like who died and made me God."

"Nearly eight billion people died. Most of them died as the result of other people. Do you understand. This whole thing wasn't about saving the now, it was about saving the future. If the world continues on its current path, there is no future. None. Sure, there be will ten years, twenty, but beyond forty or fifty?" He shook his head. "None."

"Things have already changed. The weapon was discharged, it took four or five billion lives already. There has to be a different path now."

"Sure. But have you been near the cities that weren't hit?" he asked. "I watched smoke rise into the sky as the people there just fought and destroyed things. Fought and destroyed," he said passionately. "It's only been a week. Imagine in a month, two … The riots are happening because people get desperate.'

"So, the answer is to take them out?"

He placed his hands on his hips and paced some. "People caused the extinction process. Like every other civilization."

"It's hard for you to see because you are basing it on the future."

"And it's hard for you to see right now because you're not." He lowered his head and took a moment. "Listen. I respect you. You are our leader in the future, and you stayed behind to let this you make the decision. Only you can do this. If you tell me to stop, the attack will not happen. But I beg you to think about it. Think about the future that you cannot see."

"Devon will have a future now."

"Of what? Violence, gangs, war, desperation. We had desperation. I didn't expect you to question it so much, but you did. The future you foresaw this."

"What do you mean?"

He held up a finger and walked away. I watched him walk back to the car, open the door and reach in. He pulled out a black bag, one I thought was his belongings. He walked back to me. "Think about your decision. I will do whatever you decide. But remember the woman before me didn't watch the world turn into a wasteland, she didn't see the savagery that erupted amongst humans over cans of soup. You, this woman before me didn't watch her people starve and send out men to try to find some inkling of food. The woman before me didn't watch her daughter and granddaughter die. This woman ..." he handed me the bag. "She did. And she sent these notebooks back for you. I will do whatever you command. I know it seems strange to you. To be thrust into this. Make the call, but make it after you give it thought."

I clasped the strap of the bag. It was heavy.

"Devon and I will head back to base. You know where to find me." He leaned down to me, kissed my cheek and left his mouth close to my ear. "You don't know me. But I know you. I love you. Whatever you decide."

"Whatever I decide, know that I will find you in four days. Whatever I decide. I will join you."

"I accept that."

He placed his hand on my shoulder, then turned and called for Devon.

The young man came back out.

"Babka will be joining us in a few days. Say goodbye, we'll part for now."

Devon quickly embraced me and kissed me on the cheek before leaving with his father.

They took the vehicle we brought, and we'd find another. I didn't worry about that.

I didn't understand what was happening. Weeks earlier I was this desperate woman, hating life, hating myself and everything around me. Wanting more than anything just to die. Now I was this woman who literally held the fate of the world in my hand.

How was that even possible?

FORTY-FOUR
TURMOIL

The notebooks weren't the only thing Miller placed in that bag. He also put that bottle in there. I guess the Vivian from the future really did think I would have issues.

While waiting on Owens to finish his 'talk' with Dan and Kate, I found a corner table in the dining room of the bed and breakfast. It was covered with a cloth to keep it dust free for the season and I lifted the cloth, then removed the overturned chair from the table.

I sat down. I heard the muffled voices of Owens, Dan and Kate.

I wondered how much disbelief they had. After the explanation we would leave to go to Fort Knox.

What would we tell them? If we told them anything at all.

A part of me just wanted to stay put. I hated not being honest, and the moment I saw Stan, I would have to tell him. No, I would want to tell him.

My hand moved over the coarse bag, feeling the edges of the notebooks. I pulled out the bottle and it was the first time I really looked at it.. Round like a coconut, it wasn't just hand carved, it was made for me.

Small designs with the name 'Vivian' were on the lower end with a date eleven years in the future and the letter 'O'.

I would assume it was from Owens.

The liquid swished around as I examined it, then I sought out a glass from the cabinet.

Not really thinking about it, I poured some and sat back down.

My mind was really full with all that was happening. I could see the notebooks through the open zipper. They reminded me of the ones that Stan wrote in.

Stan.

How I wish I could just pick up the phone and talk to him. He was such a plethora of wisdom, surely he could help me sort through my decision.

Why was I even worried about the decision? Why wasn't it a no brainer?

At first it was. My gut instinct was to fight for the human race, the one in the here and now. My future self was also fighting for the human race, the one that should and hopefully would exist long after I left the earth.

I didn't see those who remained as a threat. I saw them as survivors that would be grateful to be alive and would ban together to create a better future.

The original time had wildfires that started the diminishing of natural resources. Miller was right, with eighty-five percent of them started by humans. Surely, without half the population they would not happen.

But would the violence cease? The famine, the wars?

We had a full base at Fort Knox and God knows how many at Cheyenne mountain, all with the finger on the trigger.

Millions of Americans remained, and they did so without leadership or incoming food sources. Power would be down if it wasn't already and fresh water would be scarce, how long would it be until things turned bad. Not like they weren't already bad.

The worst parts of my imagination envisioned a Mad Max world, with lawlessness and violence.

Perhaps the nuclear war was thwarted but did that mean damage could not be done.

Was it possible to not detonate the weapon and still save the world? Honestly, was it ending the grim future that Miller lived or just stalling it for Devon's generation?

Maybe just maybe not detonating was the thing to do.

Maybe mankind learned its lesson and would make a better world.

Every time I knew stopping it was the right decision, suddenly I was coming up with reasons why it was the wrong decision. I had to stop thinking of the 'why we should' and focus on why we shouldn't.

My eyes shifted down to the bag.

What did I know? What did I see that made me come to the decision in the first place?

I reached in lifting the first notebook. It was dated two years and the future. It was worn and crinkled, almost as if it had been rolled up a number of times.

I flipped open the cover and to my surprise, was a note from Stan.

Viv,

Here you go. To get you started. I promise you this is a good idea for you. When you're sad or angry, or Bertha (Not sure what her name is, you told me lots of times) when she picks on you, write it out. And see, I started you out and wrote the first entry. It proves you don't always need a clean slate to make a difference. Stan.

That entry made me smile and I sipped my beverage as I turned the page.

"Viv," Owens called my name with question. "Um, you know it's not even nine in the morning, right?"

"What?"

He nodded at the glass.

"Oh., I didn't sleep much so it doesn't count."

"So, do you think your future son jump started your mood stabilizer addiction by giving you that? I mean I can't see you drinking in prison unless you were a hooch queen."

"What ... is hooch."

"Prison wine," he said. "Bet the Viv that did time knows that."

"We'll find out." I lifted the notebook.

"What's that?"

"Pretty much my life story. I wrote everything down.

"Did you read anything you wrote?" he asked.

"Not yet. Maybe later."

"You okay?"

"Yes."

"No, you're not. Don't bullshit me, lying is not a good foundation for a relationship," he joked.

"Well, we don't know if we are in one. It's not been said." I put the notebook in the bag along with the bottle, finished the drink and zipped the bag. "How did Dan and Kate handle the news?"

"Still in disbelief, like us, you know. They don't have a kid at stake."

"Tell me about it. Even though we don't know him, we will," I said. "Makes it so hard. Did you think about what we are gonna tell Fort Knox?"

"Please don't hate me." Owens lifted his hands as if in surrender. "I don't want to tell them. I mean, I don't want to tell them where they are. The future stuff they won't believe, they are just gonna attack. It makes me feel so fucking unamerican for thinking that way."

"I don't hate you. I don't want to tell them either. I want to just go. Leave, not have to face them. If it wasn't for Stan, I would. I'm gonna join them, but I won't do it without Stan."

"Or me?"

"Well, eventually we'll have to meet up."

"I don't have anybody," Owens said. "You, Kate, Dan, the others. But I'm a soldier and I am so torn."

"I know, me too."

"It's a really tough situation—"

"They're gonna detonate again," I cut him off. I didn't want to tell him but I didn't think it was right for him not to know. "That's why Devon was so scared of dying. He was afraid he'd be here, they'd detonate, and he'd die."

"Wait ... they're discharging it again?"

I nodded. "In order to achieve the goal of eliminating the threat to the future, they have to finish what they started, and they have another fifteen percent to eliminate."

"Jesus. We have to stop them."

"Do we?"

"What?" Owens asked shocked. "Yes. Are you saying we shouldn't?"

"I'm saying, we need to think about it."

231

"That's insane."

"And that was my first thought. Miller said unless the population drops it will solve nothing, there will be no future. Man will destroy himself anyhow."

"No. No." Owens shook his head and spoke strongly. "That's total bullshit. You know that. Man will persevere. The few that remain …"

"Few? It's billions that remain. Billions. That's a lot of people and a lot of damage. They're already rioting." I found the exchange to be similar to mine with Miller. It was odd. What was wrong with me?

"It's a riot, it's not a second apocalypse," Owens snapped. "We'll save our son and grandson and as many as we can. We need to get word to Miller, because once we tell Fort Knox—"

"We don't need to tell Fort Knox."

"Yes, we do. The weapon is on a ship, right? The only way to stop them is to destroy it and Fort Knox can get in touch with Cheyenne…"

"Owens no. I can stop them." I stepped to them. "Miller told me I could. I just need to say the word."

"Then say the word, Viv. There should be no question. None whatsoever," he snapped angrily. "Get your priorities straight then get your future bag. We're leaving." Owens spun and stormed out, leaving me in an air of hostility.

FORTY-FIVE
TURN AROUND

Owens was mad. Not only was he pissed over our disagreement he was fired up even more because I let Miller take our only vehicle.

Thankfully, after some walking we found another, and we were on our way.

The ride was quiet, too quiet.

Dan drove. Kate sat next to me staring out the window, her assault rifle between her legs, the butt of it on the floor as she clasped it in both hands. It looked dangerous to me, but she was the professional. Neither of them, Dan nor Kate, knew what was said between Owens and I. They probably were in their own thoughts, digesting what they had been told.

They had to feel the tension in the car. It was really thick. Maybe they didn't notice. The only talking was Owens' repeated attempts to get through to base.

"You've been trying a while," I said. "Is that normal to not answer."

"They aren't all dead if that's what you're wondering or hoping," Owens said.

"What the fuck, you dick."

"Hey, hey now." Dan called out. "No name calling. Owens is probably frustrated."

Kate interjected. "And it is common, once we hit closer to seventy miles we should make contact."

"We're in that range." Owen brought his radio to his mouth. "This is ST One, come in." Pause. "This is ST One. Come …" he lowered the radio and his head turned to the right. "I thought we weren't going near Louisville."

Dan smirked. "Your sense of direction is off. We aren't anywhere near Louisville. That's farther north. We're still sixty miles out of Fort Knox, that's something else."

"What is up ahead?" Owens asked.

"I don't know. Maybe it's more rioting."

"It's not Miller, I can say that," Owens stated.

Dan gave an upward nod. "Try the radio again, we should be getting a signal. Exit for Thirty-One is ahead."

I tilted toward the middle to see out the windshield and the sign that indicated we had a mile to the exit. The one that would take us on the final leg to Fort Knox.

I didn't see the smoke Owens referenced, and I didn't want to ask him.

As we neared it, the radio finally crackled.

"In," the male voice said. There was a pause. Then I recognized Aberdeen's voice. "This is Fort Knox calling ST One, come in."

Owens lifted that radio without hesitation. "This is ST One, we copy."

"ST One, listen," Aberdeen said. "We tracked you coming back."

Immediately, when I heard that, I cringed, I forgot about the tracking.

"We're guessing you didn't find them," Aberdeen said. "Listen go back to One-One-Seven Goleman Road. We evacuated several people in time. Sent them there."

"Evacuate? In time for what?"

"We've been overrun by insurgents. They've taken over base. Do not return."

The second that was said, Dan blasted out, "Shit." At first I thought it was a comment geared toward what we were told, then he slammed on the brakes. "Hold on."

The brakes squealed loudly. I could feel us trying to stop, then he jolted the wheel hard to the left as if trying to avoid something.

"How many are there?" Kate asked from the back.

"I don't know," Dan said. "All over the highway."

The tail end of the car spun out. We didn't immediately go into a one-eighty. The momentum of the rushed hard turn sailed me to the right and ejected my body like a rocket As soon as I landed into Kate, all glass on the passenger's side of the car shattered when rapid fire reigned upon us.

The fear was there, and adrenaline pumped. But I had lost my breath, winded from smacking into Kate. She didn't move. 'Oh God, don't let her be shot."

"Go. Just go. Keep going!" Owens ordered.

I couldn't see anything. I didn't know what was happening, why we slowed down and hadn't really moved. I felt like a rag doll, my neck was bent in an awkward position.

The car jolted; Dan gassed it.

With the tires screaming, shots fired at us without stopping, Dan brought the car around to go the other way.

I was ready to move, sit up, check on Kate …

"Watch!" Owens yelled.

Dan jerked the wheel, this time to the right. The hard turn flipped me back and sent me to my side again, this time Kate flew toward me.

I caught glimpse of her wide open eyes, her bloody face, but none of that horrified me as much as her rifle, which landed on my chest, the muzzle point blank at my nose. It landed on me a split second before the weight of her body sandwiched it between us.

Her lips moved. Her head and her body did a subtle twitching.

Mortified and scared for my life, that rifle screamed at me.

It was a second, maybe less, I reacted fast. Grabbing it by the barrel, I moved it to the left and out of the way.

Exhaling, I felt better and then she jerked her body.

Bang.

Ringing.

Black.

FORTY-SIX
PASS THE BUCK

It was the second time in a short period that I found myself drifting in and out of consciousness. Drifting between life and death. Voices surrounding me, no sense of time or how long I was out between black outs. It could have been minutes, hours, or days like with my overdose.

The feeling was the same.

Except I didn't want to die, and I couldn't figure out what was happening.

Just like with the pills, I didn't have any pain.

None.

So why did I keep blacking out?

My answers came from listening and feeling the energy around me. Coming to and just trying to capture the moment to find out what was happening.

What happened?

I heard the gun go off and the ringing in my ear and my next memory was hearing a frantic Owens blasting to Dan. *"Drive. Just drive as fast as you can."*

"Where?"

"You know where."

"Are they ..."

"Drive."

I no longer felt the weight of Kate, but Owens had jumped in the back seat. I didn't see him, I didn't see anything. But I could feel him, smell him.

Out again.

"Where is he!" Owens wasn't near me, his voice was distant. *"Get him now! Now!"*

We weren't moving at that point.

"Alright, Viv." Dan said gently near me. *"Just hold on."*

"Miller!" Owens was yelling. *"Miller Stanley … Owens, whatever the fuck you go by!"*

"Hold on, Viv."

I believed at that second I was starting to come to. My senses, kicking in.

I heard the car door open.

"Oh my God," said Miller. *"Get her inside."*

Owens brought me to Miller. He brought me to my son in hopes to help.

Was it me? Or was it Kate or both of us.

I was out again, until voices seeped into my conscious alerting me

"I'm sorry, we lost her," an unknown male voice said. At first I thought they were talking about me, until he said, *"But we've stabilized Vivian."*

Oh my God, Kate was dead? Was that what he was saying?

"We have surgical supplies; we're trying to get a room prepped to standards. We don't want infection."

"There's a hospital, two blocks away," Owens said. *"Tell me what you need. I'll get it."*

"Two blocks away? Only two blocks away?"

Then I heard Miller's voice. *"I'll get a generator. Do we have time to take it down there?"*

The strange voice replied, *"Yes, she stabilized, but I still have repair work."*

The talking grew muffled sounding, faint. I didn't know if it was the ringing in my ear that returned, or I was slipping farther away.

It happened fast, I was moving fast, suddenly I was feeling pain with every bump and jolt. I couldn't pinpoint where.

In and out of awareness.

"Vivian, I'm here," Stan said.

It was that moment that I opened my eyes. The light behind him made him look like a shadow.

"There you go. There you are. Got yourself in a pickle, didn't you? You'll be alright."

"We're taking her in."

And that was it.

The next thing I knew I was dreaming. I was in my bed, in my home, reading a book when the alarm clock went off.

Beep. Beep. Beep.

I reached over to shut it off.

Beep. Beep. Beep.

It wouldn't turn off. The oddest lucid thought hit me, had they sent me back in time?

Beep. Beep. Beep.

And then I woke up.

My senses kicked in, I could smell cleaner, hear the hum of the generator and realized the beeping was the heart monitor.

The room was dark, but I caught glimpse of a hint of light through the corner of my eye. Turning my head, I saw Stan sitting in a chair, a gooseneck lamp with yellow tint bulb bent over the notebook he was reading. He flipped a page, looked up and saw me.

"Oh my God, you're awake." He rushed over to the bed. "Not gonna say we thought we lost you. We didn't. The doctors are pretty good. Never a question. Now I'm suppose to press some button …" he looked down to the bed. "Where is it?" He lifted the covers some. "Oh, yep, you're laying on it." He found a controller and pressed it.

I pursed my lips and they felt sticky.

"You thirsty?" Stan asked. "I've been dabbing those lips with water. Wait for the doctor before you sip anything."

When I spoke the words, "What happened?" Barely anything above an audible whisper came out.

"Yeah, um, don't try to speak yet. They don't think there's any damage to the vocal cords, the bullet went straight through. It's a miracle," Stan said. "Passed through your neck, behind the windpipe and missed every artery. I'll tell you, Viv, if taking a bottle of pills with a vodka chaser and being shot twelve times doesn't tell you you're supposed to be alive, I don't know what will."

"Twelve?"

"I told you not to talk. Speaking of vodka and pills, Renee is still pissy."

That almost made me laugh.

"She's awake?" Owens said surprised.

I turned my head, it hurt to do so. Owens stood in the door and walked to the bed.

"Yeah, there's your future Romeo." Stan held up the book. "Notebook four, I think. Heck of a life you have. Enjoyed reading about your prison encounters and fights. You found your voice in notebook three. No dig to not having your voice now."

"I was talking to the doctor," Owens said. "He got the call bell. He'll be right in."

"She needs some water. I'll go find him and let you fill her in," Stan said. "I'll be back." He walked around the bed and paused by Owens. "Just so you know, your future husband never left your side. Well, a couple times, not for long."

"Thanks, Stan," Owens grumbled then walked over to me. "Glad to see you up. They thought the sedative would last until morning."

I struggled to move my mouth.

"You're thirsty, I can see that." He lifted a glass of water from the bed and aimed the straw at my lips. "A little sip won't hurt. The bullet didn't hit your esophagus. Slow, okay?"

I brought the water into my mouth, then let it rest there for a few seconds, before slowly swallowing it. My throat didn't hurt, but swallowing was difficult. Like I had a lump in my throat.

"Your voice will come back fully." He set down the water and pulled up a chair.

"Twelve?" I eeked out. "Shot twelve times."

Owens nodded. "We all got shot. You and Kate, the worst. We were a bloody mess when we got here. The big hit you took was the throat. Every shot you took came from Kate. They passed through her into you. Most of them were

241

superficial. They had like four that were in you, not deep though."

"Kate …"

He shook his head. "So many people were on the highway. I couldn't imagine there would be so much uprising so soon."

"How … many days until … Miller…"

"Until they detonate?"

I nodded.

Owens lowered his head and lifted his eyes to me. "You've been sedated for a week."

I didn't need to say a word. Owens knew hearing that shocked me when the heart monitor beeped faster.

I could feel it in my chest, the heaviness, a sudden sense of failure.

"What happened?"

"I made the decision, Viv. When you couldn't, they looked to me. I did. I … didn't take it lightly. You know. I listened to what you said about thinking about it. I started reading your journals, the later ones after prison. I made the decision. Two days after you were shot, they were closing in here. NORAD said that the untouched cities were bad, all of this in ten days. Ten days from the pulse and it fell apart. They say every society is three days away from anarchy and revolution."

"Nine," I corrected.

"Stan says it's three and after seeing all this, he's right," Owens said.

I knew by the way he spoke, the way he talked what the final decision was.

"Viv, listen. We blasted over the radio for people to get below, we blasted to wear earbuds. It was steady and continuous. We gave warning."

"Cheyenne?" I asked, knowing Fort Knox fell, but they didn't.

"They were getting ready to fire upon the Russians. It took a lot not to let loose that nuclear war four years early. They're on a skeleton crew and only had means to push a button. Thank God they didn't."

"So, it's over?"

Owens shook his head. "Not by a long shot. They still can push that button at anytime. It's a matter of wait and see. But you know what. What's done is done. Get strong and rest. We have a long road ahead."

Rest.

I didn't really have a choice at that moment. Physically, I would do so. Emotionally, how could I?

It wasn't done.

Like Owens has said …

Not by a long shot.

FORTY-SEVEN
FOR THE FUTURE

Los Angeles never burned. That entire section of California that was the catalyst for the end, didn't materialize.

We waited and watched. Hoping one devastating thing was thwarted.

It was. I supposed a lot would be and some wouldn't.

It was the first anniversary of the second pulse, and I sat on the floor of my bedroom, the journals neatly stacked around me. It was my go to place to think, to be alone, to read.

I needed to on this day.

I spent a lot of time studying my journals. Reading them as if history lessons, trying to learn something from the mistakes of the future.

In the first few months following the pulse, we gathered supplies and cleaned up, settling in Franklin Tennessee. It took several weeks for those who remained on the ship to make it to us and even longer for the woman and children from the plane to even remotely be agreeable. The first couple months were a struggle.

I actually wanted to go south for the winter, but Miller and his people knew how to survive the cold.

No surprise there.

We stayed put.

When I was distraught or complaining about cold, I pulled out a notebook. I read the hardships.

I had thirty some years to read. Admittedly I skipped stuff.

There was stuff I didn't want to know, like about Owens. If I were going to end up with that man, I wanted to get to know him on my own not from my future notes that brought up too many times how he complained about missing peanut butter.

Stan was right. I found my voice in the notebooks. My writing went from vague to that of almost a professional writer.

It was probably my way to pass the time in jail.

It was also my way to pass the time in the present. It didn't matter if I told myself just a page, I got lost in a world that was fiction to me. There was a disconnect from it, even though I wrote it.

'*Her eyes had lost the life three days ago,*' the journal entry read. '*I keep praying for something to happen. For a deep breath that would suddenly heal and make my baby better. That she would smile for me and not struggle to hold on. She's doing it for her own baby. At least I'll have a bit of my child in her own child.. I can't lose her. I can't, but I will. My daughter, my precious daughter. Please don't leave me.*'

It was heartbreaking to read. My daughter was twenty four, she had avoided catching the virus that took so many women.

The knock at the door, caused me to look up from my floor seat.

"Come in," I called out.

The door opened in Stan poked in his head. "Hey, things start in thirty minutes. You ready?"

"Yeah."

"No, you're not."

"I will be."

"Don't make me send Owens up," he said.

"Won't matter, he'll come up."

"See you down there. Get dressed."

I crinkled my brow. "I am dressed."

Grumbling a 'hmm' Stan said, "Stay sober'

"Look at you, calling the kettle black."

Stan smiled and pulled the door closed as he retreated.

He was right, I needed to get below. There was a ceremony. It would be a solemn one to celebrate the new life and to remember those that were sacrificed.

I would stay for that ceremony, but I would skip the evening festivities.

I couldn't celebrate it, not yet.

Another knock came to the door, and I knew who it was.

My knee hurt as I stood from the floor. An ache I supposed would always be there. I rubbed it, feeling the scar that along with the pain would be a reminder of the bullet that struck me.

Owens stepped in. "We need to be down there."

"I know. Go on, I'll be there, I want to pick these up."

"I'll help." He bent down for them. "Anything good?"

"You tell me, you read them all."

"I'm stocking up on peanut butter."

I laughed.

"Is that what you're wearing?"

I didn't answer, I just started at him.

"Not judging." He lifted his hands. "How are you?"

"I'm okay. You?"

"Okay, I guess." He shrugged. "It is what it is."

I hated when he took that attitude because I knew it wasn't true.

We barely spoke about it, but we would.

I thought back to that day quite a lot. The day I was told I had to choose about the weapon. For some reason I thought if we unleashed another pulse that it would be over with. I didn't think about those who remained, those who wanted to fight over what was lost.

I couldn't say that I wouldn't fight if I wasn't in the position or had the knowledge that I had.

So many people fought.

The insurgency early on was nothing compared to what it grew into. Those who refused to join us. And there was many. I often wondered if it was because a lot more people lived than had they not been given a warning.

I wouldn't have given warning if I made the decision.

The decision had been inadvertently taken from me. A decision to move forward with the weapon detonation, to remove the remaining threat to mankind's extinction. Despite the fact that he put forth effort in saving as many as he could, the burden of that decision weighed heavily on Owens. I could see it in his face, the way he would often drift off in thoughts.

It would be a burden he'd carry for a long time.

We'd both carry it.

A billion dead on our call. To ensure a green world that is plentiful and safe for generation after generation. To save a future we will never live to see. A future that almost *wasn't*.

A future originally on its way to a gray, bleak, existence void of life.

I just hope, in the end, for the sake of the future, the decision was worth it.

I know it will be. I just know it.

ABOUT THE AUTHOR

Jacqueline Druga brings to you the world's end in every way imaginable through the pages of her novels.

While best known for her apocalyptic works, Jacqueline's works expand many genres, including Humor, YA, Romance, Sci-fi and Thriller.

Jacqueline prides herself on being down to earth and lighthearted.

A mother and grandmother, Jacqueline absorbs and loves every single moment that she is writing and invites you to share in her world.

Facebook: @jacquelinedruga
Twitter: @gojake
www.jacquelinedruga.com

Printed in Great Britain
by Amazon